"If you're going to be running around the Hollingsworths' mansion," Chris said, "That means *I'm* going to be left in charge of the children, Michelle and Nicole!"

"Precisely," Susan said with a devilish smile.

"But Sooz!" Chris wailed. "I don't even *know* them! How will I even be able to tell who's Nicole and who's Michelle?"

"Don't worry, Chris. I'll fill you in on every single detail I can think of. It'll be a breeze pretending you're me."

Chris still looked doubtful.

"Look, it's not as if we've never done this before!"

THE DOUBLE DIP DISGUISE

Cynthia Blair

FAWCETT JUNIPER • NEW YORK

RLI: <u>VL: Grades 5 & up</u>
       IL: Grades 6 & up

A Fawcett Juniper Book
Published by Ballantine Books
Copyright © 1988 by Cynthia Blair

Library of Congress Catalog Card Number: 88-91158

ISBN 0-449-70256-1

Manufactured in the United States of America

First Edition: December 1988
Second Printing: July 1989

One

"*And to our graduates, the members of this year's* senior class, I offer these parting words: Congratulations . . . and good luck!"

With a smile and a nod, the principal of Whittington High School stepped off the large wooden platform that had been set up at one end of the football field. Susan Pratt and her twin sister, Christine, two of the students whose graduation from high school had just been made official on this warm sunny Saturday in the middle of June, broke into spontaneous applause. Soon everyone had joined in, the most enthusiastic being the twins' friends and classmates, who sat around them on the rows of folding chairs that lined the football field, wearing long blue robes and freshly shined shoes along with their proud smiles.

As the applause started to die down Chris and Susan turned to face each other.

"Gee, Sooz," Chris couldn't resist teasing the moment she caught sight of her twin's face, "are you developing hay fever all of a sudden, or do I actually see tears in your eyes?"

Susan laughed. "I'm afraid you're right, Chris. You know what a cornball I always am about this kind of thing."

Instead of teasing her further, however, Chris grew pensive, her dark brown eyes clouding up for a moment. "As a matter of fact," she admitted, "I'm feeling a little bit choked up myself. After all, high school graduation *is* one of the most important occasions in a girl's life."

"It is kind of sad, isn't it?" Susan thought for a few seconds. "Now that our senior year is over, we won't be seeing all our friends every day."

"Or going to committee meetings or swim meets after school."

"Or taking classes with our favorite teachers." Susan ran her fingers through her thick shoulder-length chestnut-brown hair and sighed as she contemplated all the things that she had once taken for granted but that would be coming to a close now that it was the end of June—and the end of her four years at Whittington High.

And then she brightened. "But just think, Chris. This is a time of beginnings, too. This *is* our 'commencement,' after all. We'll be moving on from here, to exciting new beginnings. We'll be doing new things, meeting new people, and then going on to college in the fall. . . ."

"You're leaving out the best part," Chris interjected with a grin.

Susan frowned. "Why, I can't imagine what you mean, Chris."

"Summer vacation!" Chris laughed. "School's out, and we have two whole months off. Yippee!"

With a chuckle Susan said, "You know, I've been so caught up in thinking about the end of school that I almost forgot about that. But you're right. We do have the entire summer ahead of us."

"And it's my favorite season! Summer means swimming and going to the beach and playing tennis and having cookouts . . . all the things I love to do most."

"You seem to be forgetting one thing, Chris," her twin reminded her.

"What's that?"

"You and I still have to find ourselves some summer jobs. We've got to start saving up for school expenses in the fall."

"Oh, that's right. I almost forgot." Chris sighed deeply, having just been reminded that July and August wouldn't be totally dedicated to outdoor sports and social events after all. "Oh, well. We'll still find time to squeeze *some* fun into our summer. After all," she added with a mischievous smile, "we Pratt twins are famous for turning even the most everyday situations into something out of the ordinary!"

It was true that Christine and Susan Pratt had become experts at adding excitement to their lives— and, more often than not, to the lives of the people around them, as well. It had all started two years earlier. The twins, then sixteen, had cooked up a scheme, nicknamed the Banana Split Affair, that was designed to allow the two girls to find out more about each other's lives. They actually traded identities, with Chris pretending to be Susan and Susan pretending to be Chris. For the truth of the matter was that while they looked identical, with their dark brown eyes, chestnut-brown hair, and upturned noses, the Pratt twins were really very different.

Chris was the outgoing one. She was always busy with her social life, constantly rushing off to visit one of her friends or getting ready to go out on a date or talking on the telephone for hours. She was also very involved with school activities. Besides being on all kinds of committees, she was a star member of Whittington High School's swim team. She loved being with people, and she loved being busy. In fact, she had found the perfect way to combine the two: while attending college in the fall, she planned to take courses that would help her prepare for a career as a lawyer.

Susan, on the other hand, was quiet and shy, preferring to spend her spare time reading, daydreaming, or, most of all, painting. Art was her true passion, and in the fall she was going to attend art school, something that had been a goal of hers for almost as long as she could remember.

Despite their differences, however, both Susan and Chris were clever and well-meaning—two traits that had on many occasions gotten them involved in all kinds of pranks and schemes that proved their courage, their creativity, and their eagerness to help other people. A year before, for example, during the time they had come to think of as Strawberry Summer, they had combined their camp counselor jobs at Camp Pinewood with a sleuthing scheme that had brought them real adventure—and kept the camp from having to close down.

"Well," Chris said as she noticed that the other seniors had risen and were starting to file out of the rows of wooden folding chairs, "hopefully our summer won't be *all* drudgery. And while it's true that neither you nor I have had any luck yet finding summer jobs, I bet we'll come up with *some* way of making money for school expenses—and maybe we'll even manage to have a good time doing it!"

"It's funny you should say that, Chris," her twin commented with a nod. "Because I, for one, intend to have *lots* of fun!"

"But in the meantime," said Chris, "let's head back to our house. Don't forget that Mom and Dad are planning a little celebration for us. And believe me: I am *ready* to celebrate!"

A half hour later, as Susan and Chris strolled into the dining room of the Pratts' house, they were surprised to see just how grand a celebration was being held in their honor. Their parents had gone all out, decorating the room with crepe paper streamers and balloons in blue and white, Whittington High's school colors. Throughout the room were pretty bouquets of fresh flowers in glass vases. And displayed in the middle of the dining room table was a special cake that had been made just for the occasion: a large rectangular one that looked like a diploma, on which was written, "Congratulations, Chris and Susan!"

It wasn't long before two dozen of the twins' cousins, aunts, and uncles had assembled there, anxious to wish the two recent graduates the best.

"Now," said Mrs. Pratt after everyone had squeezed around the table, sitting on kitchen chairs and stools and even the piano bench but somehow managing to fit comfortably all the same, "before we pour the coffee and cut the cake, why don't you two guests of honor start working on that pile of graduation presents over there?"

"Oh, are those for us?" Susan pretended to be surprised as she glanced over at the colorful stack of gaily wrapped gifts tucked away in one corner of the room.

"Well, if they are for us," her twin quipped, "I don't plan to put off opening them for another minute!"

The two girls enjoyed opening their presents, squealing with delight as they unwrapped each, then passing it around for everyone else to look at. There were two pen-and-pencil sets from their father's mom and dad, their grandparents in Vermont. They received two huge leather-bound dictionaries from their friends the Petersons, who ran the bookstore in Whittington. And from their parents there was a beautiful wristwatch for each twin: a colorful, sporty one for Chris, a delicate gold one for Susan.

The girls also read aloud the cards that so many of their relatives had sent, mail that Mrs. Pratt had been putting aside as it arrived during the days before the twins' graduation.

"Last but not least," Mrs. Pratt finally said with a smile. She glanced over toward the corner. Where previously there had been an impressive stack of presents and cards, now only one pink envelope was left. "Girls, this is from my mother and father, your other grandparents."

"Oh, good!" Susan clapped her hands gleefully. "Let me see that. Why, we haven't seen Grandma and Grandpa Stevens since . . . well, not for a long time!"

Eagerly she reached for the envelope and tore it

open. In it was a card that had a picture of a bouquet of flowers on front and a congratulatory poem inside. There was also a letter folded up and tucked inside the envelope.

"Oh, look! It's a note from Grandma!"

"Read it out loud, Sooz."

With a nod, Susan began to read the letter while the rest of her family listened attentively.

"Dear Chris and Susan," she began. "Your grandfather and I are so pleased that you two are graduating from high school this month. Congratulations! It's difficult to believe that you girls are so grown-up already.

"Thinking about how quickly time is passing has reminded us of how long it's been since we've seen you both! This summer Grandpa Stevens and I have decided to rent a cottage by the seashore, on a resort island off the coast of North Carolina called Seagull Island. The house is small, with only two bedrooms, but it has a large front porch, perfect for sitting in a rocking chair in the cool evenings. And the best part is that it's very close to the beach. It's also within walking distance of the island's small town. Seagull Village is really just a row of tiny stores, but it's large enough to supply everything we summer people might need."

"It sounds lovely!" Mrs. Pratt interjected. "Like something from a picture postcard!"

"And I'm glad that your parents have decided to take a real vacation once and for all," said Mr. Pratt. "Bill and Rosemary deserve a break."

"Ooh, wait!" Susan's cheeks had become flushed, and her brown eyes were shining. "Here's the best part! Wait until you hear this!"

"Let me see, Sooz!" Chris snatched the letter away from her sister. She took a few seconds to read the last paragraph, then whooped. "Oh, boy! Sooz, you and I are going to Seagull Island!"

"Whoa—hold on there!" At this point the twins' father reached over and took the letter.

As he skimmed it, Mrs. Pratt smiled across the table at her two daughters. "It sounds as if you two have gotten an invitation from your grandparents."

"You hit the nail on the head," said Mr. Pratt. "Your folks say that their graduation present to Susan and Chris is an all-expense-paid trip to Seagull Island for a visit—for as long as the girls want to stay, in fact."

"Can we spend the summer there?" Chris squealed. "Oh, please! Mom? Dad? *Can* we?"

Mr. and Mrs. Pratt eyed each other warily.

"I don't know," said Mr. Pratt. "I thought we'd all decided that this summer you girls would both get jobs."

"That's right," Mrs. Pratt agreed. "With both of you going off to college in the fall, it's important that we all pool our resources. It's going to be quite expensive, after all. Textbooks for Chris, art supplies for Susan, not to mention tuition . . ."

"I'm afraid you girls won't be able to spend the summer soaking up the sun and frolicking in the waves after all." Mr. Pratt was half teasing and half serious. "I'm sorry to disappoint you. But maybe you could squeeze in a weekend visit, at least."

"That sounds like fun!" Susan said brightly. "After all, a short visit is better than no visit at all."

"It would be great to see Grandma and Grandpa,"

8

Chris agreed. "A weekend visiting them on Seagull Island will give us something to look forward to."

"Now, how about getting down to some of that chocolate cake?" Mr. Pratt boomed, anxious to take his daughters' minds off whatever disappointment they might be feeling over having had the fantasy of a summer on a resort island quickly cut short to a mere weekend visit.

"You mean that cake is *chocolate* underneath all that beautiful frosting?" Chris picked up her fork, ready for a taste, her momentary regret having already faded. "Let's dig in, then! After all, I'm ready to celebrate . . . and as far as I know, there aren't many better ways to celebrate than with chocolate cake!"

The entire matter of Seagull Island was dropped until late that night, after the twins had spent the evening continuing their celebration by going to three different graduation parties, all given by friends of theirs in the Whittington High School senior class. Susan was in her room, getting ready to go to sleep. In fact, she was dressed in her pink flowered cotton nightgown, all ready to climb into bed, when she heard a cautious knock on her door.

"Chris, is that you?" she called softly. "Or has a friendly mouse come to live in our house?"

Chris let herself into the bedroom. She was wearing the oversized Whittington High T-shirt that was her nightgown these days. "If it's a mouse, it's a pretty big mouse," she replied, settling into her sister's rocking chair.

Susan glanced over and saw that despite her teasing retort, her twin was wearing a pensive frown.

"What's the matter, Chris? Can't sleep? Are you still too wound up after all the fun we had tonight? Not that I blame you, after listening to all the wild loud music the rock band over at Holly's house was playing until midnight."

Chris smiled. "Yes, is was fun, wasn't it? A little sad, maybe, since tonight was the last time we'll all have been together as members of the same high school class. . . . But to tell you the truth, the reason I can't sleep is that I've been thinking about the future, not the past."

"The future?" Susan sat down on the edge of her bed and blinked.

"Well, the *near* future. This summer, to be exact."

"Oh." Suddenly, Susan grew serious, too. "It's funny. I was really looking forward to this summer before—even the prospect of finding an interesting summer job. But ever since we got that invitation from Grandma and Grandpa Stevens, I've been wishing there were some way we could manage to go to Seagull Island for more than just a weekend. . . ."

"Funny you should say that, Sooz."

Chris leaned forward in her chair, wearing a mischievous smile. Her brown eyes were gleaming so brightly that her twin knew right away that she had come up with one of her brainstorms.

"Uh-oh. What kind of scheme have you dreamed up *this* time?" Susan teased.

"I haven't come up with any 'scheme,' Sooz. Honest. What I came up with just now is so ingenious, so obvious. . . . Well, to tell you the truth, I'm a little bit ashamed that I didn't think of it sooner."

"Christine Pratt!" Susan cried, nearly leaping off her bed. "What on earth are you *talking* about?"

10

Chris smiled and leaned back in the rocking chair. "Why couldn't you and I get jobs on Seagull Island this summer?"

Susan's jaw dropped open. She thought for a few moments . . . then burst out laughing. "You're absolutely right, Chris! Why *couldn't* we?"

"Listen, here's my plan. First we'll check with Mom and Dad. Then we'll clear it with Grandma and Grandpa. We'll head out to Seagull Island right away—as soon as we can pack, as a matter of fact. And then the minute we get there, or maybe after spending at least a couple of days soaking up the sun and relaxing, we'll start looking for jobs. That way we can easily combine summer fun with earning money!"

"That's inspired, Chris! And I bet that in a resort area like Seagull Island, you and I would have a much better chance of finding summer jobs!"

"And fast, too!"

"And I bet we can find jobs that are really interesting at a place like that!"

"Ooh, I'm already getting excited!" Chris cried. "I can hardly wait to tell Mom and Dad about this! Maybe we should go talk to them right now! . . ."

Susan couldn't help laughing as she glanced at the clock on the table next to her bed. "Chris, it's two o'clock in the morning! Somehow I doubt that they'd appreciate being woken up in the middle of the night, no matter *how* inspired your idea may be!"

"Okay, then. First thing tomorrow. And speaking of it being the middle of the night," drawled Chris, lazily pulling herself up out of the rocker, "I'm suddenly starting to feel as if I'm all partied out. I don't know about you, Sooz, but *I'm* ready to go to sleep!"

"*Sleep!* How can you possibly think about *sleep* at a

time like this?" Susan was only half joking as she watched her twin sister amble toward the door. "After all, it's very possible that in just a few days, you and I will be beginning a thrilling summer adventure on Seagull Island!"

Even as she climbed into bed a minute or two later, however, after saying good night to Chris and turning out the light beside her bed, Susan had no idea how true her teasing words would turn out to be.

Two

"Just look, Chris!" cried Susan, *rushing over to the* side of the Seagull Island ferry so that she was standing next to the railing. "Have you ever seen such a magnificent view in your entire life?"

Her twin sister, right behind her, was equally impressed.

"It's pretty incredible, isn't it?" Chris agreed breathlessly. "Why, this place *does* look like a picture postcard come to life—just like Mom said!"

It was true. The girls' first glimpse of Seagull Island was an impressive sight, something they would not soon forget. The island seemed to appear out of nowhere as the ferryboat suddenly turned around one of the bends along the irregular coastline of the mainland. Atop the high cliffs that elevated the small piece of land, the island was lush and green, covered with trees and plants that made it seem like the coolest, most refreshing place on earth, especially on a hot day in late June like this one.

Dotting the greenery were houses, both summer homes and year-round residences. Some were small and modest. But many were large Victorian houses, painted in pretty pastel shades, soft pinks and greens and blues, with turrets and widow's walks and gingerbread trim that made them look like something out of a storybook.

As the boat neared the island, one of those houses in particular caught Susan's eye. It was set apart from all the others, perched on top of a tall, lonely cliff. But its solitude was only part of it. There was something gloomy about this house, despite the beauty of its architecture. Maybe because it was painted a solemn gray, maybe because it was partially hidden by the huge trees that surrounded it . . . at any rate, just looking at it made a shiver run down Susan's spine.

"Look at *that* house, Chris!" Susan said, pointing. "Why, it looks as if it's *haunted*!"

"Or at least as if it has some wonderful story behind it," Chris said, her eyes shining as she began to let her imagination run free. "Something mysterious, some terrible secret that's been in the family for ages . . ."

"Or on second thought, maybe it's just a big gray Victorian house that belongs to some very nice people." Susan laughed, but she couldn't help feeling as if Chris's assessment of the house might be a lot more accurate than hers.

But this was no time to dwell on the possible secrets of a huge house, however beautiful and mysterious it might be. The ferry was about to dock, and the twins were eager to see Seagull Island—and, of course, their grandparents.

A few minutes later, as soon as they had filed off the boat with the other passengers who'd traveled across to the island from the mainland, they caught sight of their host and hostess for the next six weeks. Bill and Rosemary Stevens were standing next to the dock with all the island residents and summer people who were there to pick up their friends and guests, both of them peering out toward the dock expectantly.

"Grandma! Grandpa!" Chris called. She waved frantically as she tried to catch the attention of the two familiar faces she had just spotted among the crowd.

"*There* they are!" cried Rosemary Stevens, rushing over to the girls. Her husband was not far behind. "Oh, it's so good to see you both!" The older woman threw her arms around Susan, then Chris, giving them each a warm, welcoming hug.

"What a treat it is to have you both here with us this summer!" the twins' grandfather said heartily. "And I must say," he added with a twinkle in his blue eyes after he had taken a moment to look at them both carefully, "you two haven't changed a bit since the last time we saw you."

"We haven't?" Susan was a bit surprised, especially since both girls' hair was now so much shorter than it had been the last time around.

"Nope. Why, you two are still as alike as two peas in a pod! Or, I should say, now that I'm a Seagull Islander," he said with a wink, "as alike as two conch shells on the beach!"

The four of them were laughing and chattering away happily as they walked over to the Stevenses' car. Chris and Susan were anxious to fill their grandparents in on all the details of their trip out from Whittington: the airplane flight, the bus ride to the dock, and finally the quick but memorable ferryboat ride over to the resort island. But they weren't so busy

15

talking that they didn't remember to take a good look at their surroundings, at this brand-new place, which was going to be their home for most of the summer.

The town of Seagull Village, just behind the dock, was indeed small, just as their grandmother had reported in her letter. But it was so charming that the twins could hardly wait for the opportunity to explore it more freely. The buildings lining Ocean Street were covered in weathered gray shingles, giving the main street a rustic air that was just perfect for a remote beach town where people went to get away from the hustle and bustle of their everyday lives. There were a grocery store, a drug store, a hardware store, and a few other businesses. And, Susan and Chris were pleased to see, there was even a small ice cream shop, the ideal place to stop for an ice cream cone after a long hot day at the beach.

"This place is terrific!" Chris exclaimed as the car veered off the island's main thoroughfare. Suddenly, instead of shops and businesses, there were summer houses on one side of the road—and a beautiful white-sanded beach on the other. "And just look at this gorgeous beach! I can't wait to get out there!"

"Me, too!" Susan agreed. "I love romping around in the waves."

"Sorry to put a damper on your plans, girls," their grandfather interjected gently, glancing at the twins through the rearview mirror, "especially when you haven't even unpacked yet. But I'm afraid that when you do finally get around to unpacking, you might as well leave your bathing suits in your suitcase."

"What?" Chris squealed. "What do you mean, Grandpa?"

Grandma and Grandpa Stevens exchanged rueful glances.

"I'm afraid that the Seagull Island beaches are going to be closed for most of the summer."

"Closed! But—but this is a *resort* island!" Chris sputtered. "Why on earth would anyone close the beaches?"

"What Grandpa is trying to tell you is that three days ago someone dumped thousands of gallons of chemical waste into Seagull Harbor." Grandma Stevens shook her head sadly. "The water in the whole area is polluted—so polluted that it's considered unsafe for swimming. And according to the reports in the *Seagull Island Gazette*, it will be weeks before it works its way out and the water is clean again."

"And if all that weren't bad enough, the local government officials haven't yet been able to figure out who's responsible." Grandpa Stevens frowned. "Someone ought to reimburse the businesses around here that cater to the tourist trade and are bound to suffer by the beaches being closed for most of the summer. And it seems that no one's been able to find out who the guilty party is, not even the *Gazette*'s top reporters."

"But that's terrible!" Susan cried. "Not only is the water being polluted, but the Seagull Island residents who make their living from the summer visitors are going to lose lots of money!"

"That's right," her grandmother agreed. "It's an awful situation—and one that's going to require some serious investigation. Whoever the culprit is, whichever company it is that's behind it all, it's high time they stood up and took responsibility for what they've done!"

"But we don't want to discourage you, girls," said Bill Stevens. "There's still plenty to do here on Seagull Island. Biking, tennis, swimming at the town pool . . . and I can't wait for you to try some of my barbecued chicken."

At that point Chris and her grandparents launched into an animated discussion of Bill Stevens's new-found talent for broiling chicken over hot coals. Indeed, all the members of the merry foursome were only too happy to put the unpleasant issue of the sudden and mysterious polluting of Seagull Harbor out of their minds.

And then the Stevenses' car pulled up into the driveway of a pleasant little bungalow white with bright blue shutters. Just as the twins' grandmother had said in her letter, the house was only a few hundred yards from a scenic stretch of beach. On one side of the large porch was a round table, along with four wooden deck chairs. And sure enough, on the other side, the one that gave the best view of the ocean, was a rocking chair, just waiting for someone to sit in it and while away the cool hours of early evening.

"Here it is," Rosemary Stevens said proudly. "Our home for the summer. And now it's your home, too."

"It's a great little house!" Chris exclaimed, and she really meant it. "It's going to be fun living here; I just know it. I can't wait to see the inside."

She and Susan weren't disappointed. While the rooms were small, all had large windows, so that the sun could come streaming in. The furniture was simple, much of it wicker, but the curtains and cushions were in fresh shades of green and pink.

Overall, it had a rustic feeling to it, just like Seagull Island itself.

"And here's your bedroom," the girls' grandmother said after she'd completed the tour of the tiny house and shown them into the back bedroom. There were cheerful yellow bedspreads on its two single beds and yellow curtains on the windows. "It's small, but it's still a very nice room, with a wonderful view of the beach."

"It's beautiful!" Chris assured her. "I love it!"

Susan, however, wasn't paying attention. She had glanced out the back window, the one that was catercorner to the one with the ocean view, and found that she had an excellent view of that house again, the one that had first caught her attention on the ferry ride over to the island.

Up close, she could see that it wasn't at all run-down as she had thought at first. And it didn't look "haunted," the way Chris had jokingly suggested. As a matter of fact, it looked as if it was very carefully kept up. The large, heavy shutters were freshly painted in black, the huge hedges surrounding the front were carefully trimmed, and the brass trim on the high black wrought iron gate had been polished until it shone.

No, whoever lives in that house certainly takes good care of it, she was thinking as her sister chattered away to their grandparents about the big plans both twins had for getting interesting summer jobs. Even so, just looking at it gives me the creeps!

Susan's attention was gradually drawn away from the house, however, as she became aware that her sister was talking to her.

"Don't you think this is a great room, Sooz?"

"Huh? Oh, uh, sure. Yes, it's a beautiful room," Susan was quick to agree.

"See? I told you Sooz had good taste, Grandma! Besides," Chris went on, casting a teasing look in her twin's direction, "since we'll be sharing a room, Sooz and I will be able to tell each other all our secrets every night. And we can fill each other in on all the exciting details of the day's adventures."

"That's right," Susan agreed with a chuckle.

"Goodness!" cried their grandfather, coming in behind the threesome. "What kind of 'adventures' are you two planning on having this summer?"

Chris and Susan looked at each other and laughed.

"To tell you the truth, Grandpa," said Chris, "we don't know yet. But there's one thing we *do* know. Given our history, we Pratt twins are bound to come up with *something*!"

Three

The twins had planned to spend at least a day or two relaxing on Seagull Island, unpacking and exploring their new home and spending some time catching up with their grandparents. But when they both awoke early the next morning, refreshed from a good night's sleep that was the result of both their long day of traveling and the fresh, salty air wafting in through the open windows of their bedroom, it turned out that they were both thinking along the same lines.

"Well, Sooz," said Chris over breakfast, after helping herself to a second serving of the waffles that she and her twin had whipped up as a surprise for their grandparents, "today is Monday, our first full day as full-fledged Seagull Islanders. What do you want to do? Go to the pool? Play tennis? Drive around the island?"

"Or you girls could join your grandmother and me in a game of golf," their grandfather offered. "Rose-mary and I have become quite good at the game, if I do say so myself. And to think we didn't even start playing until a couple of weeks ago."

"Now, Bill," Rosemary Stevens scolded him gently, "I thought we'd agreed to let our daily golf game go for a while, at least until the twins got settled in here." Turning to her granddaughters, she explained, "I'm afraid we've become dedicated golfers in a very short time. Especially your grandfather."

"That's right. In fact, the only time we miss a game is when it rains. And so far that's only happened twice."

"Oh, please don't give up something you love so much just because we're here!" Susan protested. "We're supposed to be living here, too, remember? We're not houseguests that you might feel you have to entertain. We don't want to get in your way!"

Bill Stevens glanced at his watch. "Well, Ro, it's not too late to squeeze in nine holes. What do you say?"

"But it's the girls' first day here!" Rosemary looked at Chris and at Susan, then back at her husband.

"Susan is right," Chris insisted. "Please, go ahead and do whatever you'd normally do. Susan and I will find some way of keeping ourselves busy. I know; after we've cleaned up the kitchen, we'll go have a look around the island."

"Are you sure?" Their grandmother still wasn't completely convinced.

"Of course!" Susan was firm. "Now, you two had better scurry out of here before that summer sun gets any hotter. I'll tell you what; we'll all meet back here at lunchtime. Okay?"

"It's a deal!" said Grandpa Stevens. "And in honor of your arrival, I'll try out that barbecue grill out back.

How does a lunch of my famous charcoal-broiled chicken sound?"

"Yum!" Chris laughed. "Already I can hardly wait for lunch!" To prove how impressive her eating capacity was, she popped a huge forkful of waffles into her mouth.

Once the girls were alone, they were still faced with the same dilemma: how to spend their first day on the resort island.

"Do you know what I'd really like to do?" Chris asked slowly, toying with her spoon. "I'd like to check out those little shops over on Ocean Street. You know, the ones we passed as we were driving here from the ferry."

"Is there something you need?" Susan asked with a frown. "Something you forgot to pack?"

"Well . . . as a matter of fact," Chris said, almost sounding as if she felt a little guilty about the confession she was about to make, "I thought maybe I'd stop in at a few of those stores and see if any of them were interested in hiring summer help."

Susan couldn't help laughing. "Why, Christine Pratt! And here I thought we'd decided to take a little *vacation* before we started looking for summer jobs!"

"Well . . . I know. But don't you feel as if just *being* here on Seagull Island is a vacation in itself?"

"To be perfectly honest, I do. And while we're telling the truth," Susan confessed, "I might as well tell you that I'm kind of anxious to start looking for a job, too."

"In that case, why don't we forget all about forcing ourselves to spend the day being idle and instead get going with what we *really* want to be doing?"

"Good idea, Chris!"

"In fact, why don't we have a contest?"

"A contest?" Susan was puzzled.

"We'll see who gets a job first!"

"You're on!" Susan stood up and began clearing the table, ready for the job-finding competition to begin. "I'll just wash these breakfast dishes. . . ."

"And I'll put these things in the refrigerator."

"But what about the winner? What's the prize?"

Chris paused for a moment, the butter dish in one hand and the milk pitcher in the other. And then a grin slowly crept across her face. "*I* know! Remember that little ice cream place we saw on Ocean Street?"

"Of course."

"Okay, then. The winner gets a free ice-cream cone—and the loser has to buy it."

"Double dip?"

"Double dip!"

"You're on, Chris!"

"Great. I just hope they have my favorite, chocolate almond chip," Chris said with a twinkle in her brown eyes. "Because *I* intend to have landed a summer job by noon today!"

A few hours later, however, Chris's optimism had all but faded. She had gone to almost every one of the dozen or so stores lining Ocean Street—with no luck whatsoever. The drug store wasn't taking anyone on. The hardware store had already hired two people for the summer. The grocery store was interested only in people with experience working a cash register. It was so discouraging!

In fact, Chris was on the verge of giving up for the morning, of walking back to her grandparents' beach house, when she noticed for the first time that despite the large breakfast she'd wolfed down earlier that morning, she was hungry again—no doubt the result of all the difficulty she'd been having accomplishing what she had expected would be a relatively simple task.

She was about to stop back in at the grocery store for a snack when she noticed that she was standing in front of the Seagull Ice Cream Emporium. True, it was kind of early in the day for ice cream, but the sun was hot, she was both hungry and thirsty . . . and besides, she just couldn't resist. Chris ducked inside the ice-cream shop, already trying to decide whether she felt like sticking to her favorite flavor or trying something new.

Inside the shop the air was cool and refreshing, mainly because of the large ceiling fan turning slowly overhead. It was a small, pleasant store, with both a take-out counter and a place for people to sit and enjoy any of the twelve flavors—all of which, according to the sign on the wall, were homemade.

As she was reading through the list of flavors posted behind the counter, Chris heard someone say in a cheerful voice, "And here comes my very first customer of the day. What'll it be? Double-dip cones are today's special. Two flavors for the price of one!"

"How about a *triple* dip?" Chris returned jokingly, realizing how difficult it was going to be to make a decision.

She turned to look at the person behind the counter and saw that it was a good-looking boy with light blond hair and blue eyes. He looked as if he was about her age, and from the big, friendly grin he was wearing, Chris got the feeling that he was someone she would enjoy getting to know better.

25

"A *triple* dip!" he repeated with a merry laugh. "Wow! Now, *that's* a lot of ice cream!"

"Yes, but that way I'd get to taste three of your homemade ice-cream flavors, instead of just two. Hey, *I* know!" Chris snapped her fingers as an idea came to her. "The Fourth of July is just a few days away, right? So how about selling a triple-dip special—red, white, and blue? You could have strawberry and vanilla. . . ."

"And black raspberry!" The boy chuckled. "That's a terrific idea! You're an ice cream genius. This place could use someone like you."

"Oh, really?" Chris smiled. "Well, it just so happens that I'm looking for a summer job, and there's nothing I'd like better than working around one of my favorite things in the whole world—ice cream! I don't suppose the Seagull Ice Cream Emporium is interested in hiring anybody right now. . . ."

"As a matter of fact," the boy said seriously, "just this morning I was talking to the owners of this place, the Coopers, about that very subject. Their niece was supposed to work here this summer, but at the last minute she had to take a course at summer school." He shrugged. "It seems to me that they'd be thrilled to have you come work here in her place. They wouldn't even have to advertise for her replacement in the *Seagull Island Gazette*. You just appeared, as if you'd been dropped down here from the heavens."

"Not exactly." Chris laughed. "Actually, I was dropped here by the Seagull Island ferry. But that doesn't mean I don't have a strong arm for scooping ice cream!"

"Well, then, as far as I'm concerned, you're hired. Here, I'll tell you what. I'll telephone the Coopers right now and tell them the good news. But there is one important question I have to ask you first."

Chris suddenly grew serious. Her mind raced as she thought of all the possible questions this boy might bring up. Have you ever worked in a store before? Do you have experience working a cash register? How well do you know the island?

"What's the question?" she asked with a gulp.

The boy grinned. "What's your name?"

She couldn't help laughing. "Christine Pratt. And for the next six weeks or so, I'll be staying with my grandparents, Bill and Rosemary Stevens. They've rented a beach house for the summer over on Shore Road."

"Great. That's all I need to know."

"Wait—it's my turn. I have *three* questions I want to ask."

"Three?" The boy looked startled.

"That's right. One is, what hours will I be working? The second is, how much will my salary be?"

"Sorry. I can't help you with either of those. I'm afraid those are details you'll have to work out with the Coopers."

"Fair enough."

"Maybe I'll have better luck with your third question."

"I certainly hope so!" said Chris with a chuckle. "Because I was about to ask you what *your* name is!"

"That's one question I *can* answer! My name is Neil Weaver. And I happen to be one of the few people who actually live on Seagull Island year round."

"Good. In that case," Chris joked flirtatiously, "since I'm still a newcomer and all, I'll consider you my official tour guide."

"It's a deal! But first, how about the ice-cream cone you wanted? It's on the house! And then I'll put that call in to the Coopers."

By noon, Chris had returned to her grandparents' beach house, just as she and Susan had agreed. Sure enough, she had a summer job all lined up, just as she'd predicted.

But she had two other things as well, neither of which she had expected. One was a stomach full of ice cream, two of the largest scoops she had ever seen in her entire life. And the other was a movie date for that same evening, with none other than Neil Weaver.

Four

While Chris had immediately headed toward the quaint shops of Ocean Street in her search for summer employment, her twin had taken a different approach. Susan had gone in the opposite direction, borrowing her grandparents' car and traveling inland, rather than toward the beach. Her grandparents had said something about a big supermarket over that way, a large, modern store that catered to the island's year-round residents, as opposed to the small places by the waterfront, which tended to be frequented by day tourists and summer renters.

There's bound to be some kind of community bulletin board in a big store like this, she thought as she pulled into the supermarket's parking lot. I have a hunch that some of the local people would use a place like that to advertise for summer help. Maybe I'll find something here. . . . At any rate, it's as good a place as any to start, especially since the next edition of the *Seagull Island Gazette* isn't due out until Thursday.

Sure enough, Susan's prediction proved correct. There was a bulletin board right inside the store's entrance. She stood in front of it, eagerly scanning the job openings that had informally been posted there, described on index cards or cardboard or little pieces of paper.

But she grew more and more dismayed as she read about each of the dozen or so jobs listed. The first was a night job, not at all the kind of thing she was looking for. The next required access to a car. The one after that, working in a bakery, sounded promising, but then she noticed it was over on the mainland, much too far to go every day. Sailing instructor, dog walker, newspaper carrier . . . none of them sounded quite right.

Momentarily discouraged, Susan turned away, shaking her head slowly and frowning. She was about to leave the store, to drive back to her grandparents' house and wait a few days for the *Gazette* to come out with its help-wanted ads in the classified section, when she noticed that a tall, good-looking boy with black hair and green eyes had just come over, carrying three or four pieces of paper and a handful of tacks. Without giving her a second glance, he began putting the paper up on the bulletin board.

"Oh, good! More jobs!" Susan said aloud, even though she was really talking to herself.

The boy looked over at her and smiled. "Looking for a job?" he asked in a friendly tone of voice. "You shouldn't have too much trouble. There's always a big demand for summer employees around here."

"Yes, but none of the jobs that are posted on this bulletin board are quite right for me."

"Well, then, maybe you'll get lucky with one of these." He gestured toward the listings he had just put up. "Here, be my guest."

"Thank you. I will have a look."

As she glanced at the board once again, the boy said, "By the way, I'm Todd Moore. If there's anything I can do to help . . . maybe even put in a good word for you with my boss. This isn't too bad a place to work for the summer. At least it's air-conditioned. And when it's really hot, all the kids who work here spend their breaks hanging out over in the frozen foods section."

Susan glanced over at Todd and chuckled. "Thanks, Todd. But I think I may have just found the perfect job for me."

"Oh, really? Here, let me see."

She pointed to the very last job listing he had tacked onto the bulletin board. On a white index card, in a neat, squarish handwriting, someone had printed carefully, "Wanted: Mother's Helper." In smaller letters was written more information about the job: "Care for two girls, ages nine and seven. Hours 8:30 to 5:30, wages competitive. Experience required." At the very bottom was a telephone number.

"Sounds good to me," said Todd with an approving nod. "I wonder who it is who's advertising. Being from Seagull Island and all, I know most of the folks around here."

"Well, you know what they say," Susan replied brightly. "There's only one way to find out!" She had already copied the telephone number into the small notebook she'd brought along precisely for that purpose. "Now, can you point me toward the nearest pay phone?"

"Sure. There's one at the back of the store."

"Good. I'll go call right now."

"Now, that's what I call eager! Hey, good luck—uh, what did you say your name was?"

"I didn't," Susan said with a shy smile. "But it's Susan. Susan Pratt."

"Okay, then. Good luck, Susan! And, uh, I guess I'll be seeing you around!"

"Maybe!" Susan waved as she headed toward the back of the store, in search of the telephone. The prospect of seeing Todd Moore again was a pleasant one. Even so, she had other things on her mind at the moment—like getting that mother's helper job. And as she dialed the telephone number, she had a feeling that this was going to turn out to be just the right job for her, never suspecting that the phone call she was about to make was going to launch her on one of the strangest escapades of her entire life.

"So, Sooz, it looks as if I won the bet!" Chris teased over lunch that same afternoon. "And not only did I get a summer job; I got one at the very same place where you're going to have to make good on that deal of ours!"

"Wait a minute, Chris," her grandfather interjected. "Susan here has a job interview lined up for four o'clock this afternoon. Surely that counts for something in this little contest of yours. . . ."

"Chris is right," Susan insisted cheerfully. "She won our contest, fair and square. Besides," she went on teasingly, "if I take her to the Seagull Ice Cream

Emporium for a cone, I'll be able to meet this new boyfriend of hers!"

"Oh, Neil isn't a boyfriend," said Chris, her cheeks pink. She looked over at her twin and with a sly grin added, "Not yet, anyway."

"Well, we've heard all about Chris's new job," said the girls' grandmother as she passed the plate of barbecued chicken that her husband had just made. "How about yours, Susan?"

"To tell you the truth, Grandma, I don't really know too much about it yet. All I know is I'm meeting a Marion Hollingsworth at four, and her address is Number One Cliffside Drive. She hardly said anything to me on the phone. I told her I was calling about the mother's helper job, and she immediately told me when and where to show up. She didn't even bother to ask me how old I was or what kind of experience I had. Kind of strange, don't you think?"

"I'd say it's kind of spooky, if you ask me," Chris commented, reaching for the potato salad.

"Oh, I'm sure there's really nothing spooky about it," Susan went on, feeling a little silly. "Marion Hollingsworth is probably just . . . efficient."

"Cliffside Drive," Bill Stevens was repeating. "Now, where exactly do you suppose that is? I seem to remember the name, somehow. You know, Ro and I went out for a drive our first day here, and we got a little bit lost. . . ."

"Now I remember!" Rosemary exclaimed. "I *thought* it sounded familiar! Why, Cliffside Drive is where that big gray Victorian house is!"

Susan felt a chill run down her spine. "*That's* where the Hollingsworths live? That house is the place where I'm going for my job interview this afternoon?"

"You've said all along that you wanted an 'interesting' summer job, Sooz," her twin said matter-of-factly. "And it looks as if that's exactly what you've found for yourself!"

"Well, now, let's not jump to conclusions," their grandmother hastened to interject. "I'm not *positive* that that's the house. . . . There must be other houses on Cliffside Drive, as well."

"We'll find out soon enough," said Chris. She was about to reach for her third piece of chicken when she noticed that her sister had stopped eating. "What's the matter, Sooz?" she teased. "Lost your appetite?"

"Oh, it's nothing," Susan replied. She was trying to sound casual, but her voice sounded thick and strange. "It's just that, all of a sudden, I'm a little bit . . . *nervous* about this job interview."

But the peculiar thing was, she didn't know if she was afraid that she *wouldn't* get a job working at the Hollingsworths' house . . . or that she *would*.

While the Victorian house on Cliffside Drive was actually walking distance from the Stevenses' beach house, Susan borrowed her grandparents' car for that afternoon's job interview. After all, she wanted to be careful not to muss the pretty green sundress she was wearing or scuff her white pumps.

As she drove slowly uphill, along the narrow, winding road that took her closer and closer to the top of Seagull Island's highest cliff, there were butterflies in her stomach. She tried desperately to talk herself out of being nervous.

In the first place, she told herself, you don't even know for certain that Number One Cliffside Drive *is* that big gray house. And even if it turns out that it is, you're just imagining that the place is eerie. It's actually a very nice house. Why, with a little yellow paint and a few pots of geraniums . . . And even if the house *does* look just a teensy bit creepy, the Hollingsworths are probably very nice people.

The butterflies were still batting their little wings with full force, however, as Susan drove up to the tall black wrought iron gate, with its brass trim and ominous-looking spikes running along the top. Sure enough, on each side was a plaque that read "Number One." She gulped, then drove inside, where there was a circular driveway whose gravel crunched beneath the tires of her car.

There were no signs of life as she walked up to the front door, only the screaming of sea gulls flying around way overhead. Susan took a deep breath before reaching for the ornate brass knocker.

The noise it made as she knocked three times seemed to echo through the stillness of the house.

It's hard to believe that two little girls live in this gloomy, silent house, thought Susan, wondering if perhaps she should just turn back and forget the whole thing. Especially when I think about all the noise and happy chaos that was always around when Chris and I were growing up.

But before she had a chance to change her mind, the door opened. A somber-looking man in a dark suit stood in the doorway, peering down at her and frowning.

"May I help you?" he asked with a perfect English accent, sounding as if he wasn't really very interested in "helping" her at all.

"I—I'm looking for Marion Hollingsworth."

"Is she expecting you?" Once again, his attitude was clear.

"As a matter of fact, she is. I'm Susan Pratt, and I have a four o'clock appointment with her." As proof, she added, "I'm here for an interview for a mother's helper position."

Boy, I bet Chris would never let a guy like that intimidate *her*, Susan was thinking as she tiptoed down the hall, following the butler but staying a few feet behind him.

The inside of the house was as impressive as the outside, both beautiful and forbidding at the same time. The wooden floors were highly polished. Elaborate crystal chandeliers hung from the ceiling. Antiques and statues that all looked as if they were valuable were tucked into every corner of the room. Even so, despite all the care that had obviously gone into this house, the air seemed heavy somehow. It was also quite dark, since thick velvet drapes covered practically every window.

"Ms. Hollingsworth will receive you in the drawing room." The butler had stopped in front of a pair of double doors, which he opened with great ceremony, leaning forward.

Susan's heart was pounding so loudly as she walked across the Oriental carpet that she was afraid the woman sitting in one corner of the large room—Marion Hollingsworth, she assumed—would hear it. But if she did, she didn't let on.

Instead, she stood up and extended her hand.

"Good afternoon, Miss Pratt," she said, looking at Susan in the same way the butler had.

Susan felt as if she were dressed all wrong, or her

shoes needed polishing, or she'd forgotten to brush her hair. But since none of those things happened to be the case, she told herself she was only feeling so self-conscious because this was the very first job interview she had ever been on in her entire life.

"Good afternoon, Ms. Hollingsworth," she said, forcing a smile.

"Please sit down." Ms. Hollingsworth smoothed the skirt of her plain black dress, which had long sleeves and a high neck. Then she perched on the edge of a straight-backed wooden chair.

While at first glance she had assumed that this woman was her grandmother's age, Susan realized, once she was sitting directly across from her, that Ms. Hollingsworth was in actuality quite young. But her dark hair was pulled back into such a severe bun, worn at the base of her neck, and her clothes were so prim that she looked much older than she really was. Susan studied her face and saw that there was only coldness reflected in the woman's dark eyes. In fact, she didn't smile once.

"The position I am looking to fill consists of watching two little girls—Nicole, who is seven years old, and Michelle, who is nine. We need someone all day, from eight-thirty to five-thirty, five days a week. Please tell me about your experience with children."

Susan kept her reply brief, telling Ms. Hollingsworth about all the baby-sitting she had done over the past four or five years. The woman listened without saying a word or even changing her expression.

By the time Susan had finished, she had decided that this woman didn't approve of her at all and would never hire her in a million years. So she was astonished when Ms. Hollingsworth stood up and said, "Now you will meet Michelle and Nicole."

"Where *are* they?" Susan ventured bravely as she followed her interviewer up a large wooden staircase and past a row of large dark oil paintings, all of them portraits of somber-looking people. "It's such a beautiful day. I'm surprised they're not outside, playing."

"Michelle and Nicole are working on their studies."

Susan was about to speak up on the little girls' behalf, protesting that it was, after all, summer vacation. But she could tell that Marion Hollingsworth was not the type of person who was interested in hearing other people's opinions.

Sure enough, as they entered a large bedroom, which was decorated mostly in white, Susan was astounded to find two little girls sitting at their desks, reading.

"Michele, Nicole, come meet Miss Pratt. She is going to be working for us this summer, taking care of you both while your father is at work and I am busy running the house."

Once again Susan was tempted to speak up, to say something about the fact that she hadn't yet decided whether or not she was really interested in working in an odd household like this one. But she concluded once again that it was best to keep silent, at least for now.

Dutifully the girls laid down the thick books they had been reading and came over to Susan. They stood before her without speaking, just staring at her and blinking.

"Now I will leave you all alone to see how you get on." Within moments Ms. Hollingsworth was gone, having slipped out into the hallway and closed the door gently behind her.

"Do you like to play games?" Nicole, the younger of the two, asked shyly.

"I love games," Susan replied, smiling at the pretty little girl, who had green eyes and long blond braids. "And I bet we could have lots of fun, playing together. What about you, Michelle? Do you like to play games?"

"Hmph." Michelle just glared at Susan, then turned away, picked up her book, and pretended to be absorbed in it.

"Oh, don't mind her," whispered Nicole. "She's always cranky." She reached over and took Susan by the hand. In a normal voice she said, "Come over to the toy box, and I'll show you my favorite dolls."

As Susan sat down on the floor beside Nicole to admire her collection of dolls, she knew that her heart had already been stolen by this charming and vivacious seven-year-old. What a sunny child she was! There was nothing that Susan would have liked better than to spend the summer taking care of her.

But then there was Michelle. The older girl continued to ignore Susan, staying off on one side of the room, not looking up from her book even once.

She's a lot like her mother, Susan thought. But then she realized that she wasn't even certain that Ms. Hollingsworth *was* the girls' mother. She certainly didn't act as if she was.

It looks as if Chris was right, she thought grimly. The family in this house *does* have secrets.

Maybe I'll ask Todd if he knows anything about the Hollingsworths, she decided. It was then that she realized that despite Ms. Hollingsworth's icy formality, despite Michelle's standoffishness, even despite the eeriness of this house, which was so badly lacking in homeyness, she was going to accept the job, if it was indeed offered to her. After all, the sweet little girl who sat on the floor beside her, chatting away happily about her dolls, obviously thrilled to have a visitor, was bound to make working here worthwhile.

As Susan was about to leave the house a few minutes later, Ms. Hollingsworth, who was seeing her to the door, said, "The girls seemed to like you very much, Miss Pratt."

"Please—call me Susan." That much, at least, she was entitled to ask for.

"All right, then. Susan. We would like you to start tomorrow morning at eight-thirty." The salary Ms. Hollingsworth offered was generous indeed, so much so, in fact, that it was all Susan could do to keep from gasping.

Wait until I tell Chris, she was thinking as she drove back down the winding road, toward her grandparents' beach house. I got a job my first day here on Seagull Island, just as she did. And I'm going to be making more money that I ever dreamed possible. It all sounds too good to be true.

It was too bad, then, that there was still something nagging at her as she drove further and further away from the Hollingsworths' house. She had so many unanswered questions. Who exactly was Marion Hollingsworth? If she wasn't the girls' mother, who was . . . and where was *she*? Why was Michelle so withdrawn and angry, a fact that was even more strange, given her sister's well-adjusted personality? And why was everything in that house so darned *gloomy*?

Maybe I'm just imagining things, she thought. Or maybe there really is something peculiar about the family who lives in that big gray house.

But since I'm now an employee of the Hollingsworths, Susan reminded herself ruefully, chances are that sooner or later I'm going to find out!

Five

"*I don't know, Susan. I'm sure you really* believe *that* the Hollingsworths are mysterious, living in that big old house on the cliff and all. . . . But I can't help feeling that you're letting your imagination run away with you just a little bit.*"

Todd Moore shook his head slowly. Then he leaned over and took half a dozen boxes of breakfast cereal out of the large cardboard carton he was unpacking and arranged them neatly on the supermarket shelves.

It was later that same afternoon, after Susan had stopped off at the Stevenses' beach house to tell Chris and her grandparents the good news about her mother's helper job. But as she told them about sweet little Nicole and her older sister, Michelle—whom she made a point of describing simply as "shy"—she couldn't help thinking about her first impression of the Hollingsworths: that there was something about them that was very peculiar indeed. And so the very first chance she got, she had rushed out to find Todd. After all, he had said himself that he pretty much knew everybody on Seagull Island. And what she was looking for at the moment was more information about the intriguing collection of people living at Number One Cliffside Drive.

"Here, let me make sure I've got this straight," he went on, pausing in his unpacking of the carton. "You called up about the mother's helper job you saw advertised on the bulletin board. And when you got to the house for an interview, you met Marion Hollingsworth, who was kind of distant—formal, not very friendly. Right?"

"Well, it was *more* than that." Now that she was talking about it all out loud, Susan was more unsure of her suspicions than ever. After all, it was true that Ms. Hollingsworth hadn't actually *done* anything out of the ordinary. . . . Everything Susan was feeling was based on nothing more than intuition. "She just seemed . . . well, not very warm, not even to her daughters. *Are* they her daughters?"

Todd scratched his head. "As far as I know. The little girls go to some private boarding school during the year, so they're not around very much. As for their mother, or whoever it is that's raising them, she keeps a pretty low profile. She doesn't go out very much. You hardly ever see her in public. It's Mr. Hollingsworth who's always in the public eye. . . .

"Listen, Susan, I don't mean to make light of your first impression of the Hollingsworths, that they might be a little strange. Maybe they are kind of eccentric. But you're talking about Seagull Island's oldest, wealthiest, most civic-minded family. The Hollingsworths' contributions are what started the town library and the scholarship fund and the park over at the edge of town. . . .

"And then there's Mr. Hollingsworth. Wait until you meet him. What a guy! He's the kind of man who serves as an example for all of us. Sure, he's a successful businessman, running the family business and all, but he always manages to find the time to go to fund-raising events and give speeches about how important it is to be a good citizen. His picture appears in practically every issue of the *Gazette*! He's friends with the mayor, knows all the businesspeople on the island. . . . In fact, Charles Hollingsworth was even the guest speaker at my high school graduation a couple of weeks ago!

"Yes, the people who live in this town owe the Hollingsworths a lot. It's hard to believe that there could actually be anything funny going on as far as they're concerned."

Susan thought for a minute. She had known that the Hollingsworths were wealthy, of course; anyone could see that. But she had had no idea that they were so prominent here on the island. From what Todd was saying, it did sound as though they were good people . . . even if they were a little bit odd.

Yes, Todd is probably right, Susan decided. I guess I am reading things into all this. They're probably very nice, very *normal* people, once you get to know them.

"Okay, then," she said aloud. "I'm willing to give them a chance. But for now . . . what time do you get off work?"

Todd glanced at the big clock on the back wall of the store. "In about three minutes," he replied with a grin.

"Well, then, how about helping me celebrate having gotten this job?"

"You're on! Where shall we go?"

Susan laughed. "Just tell me one thing, Todd. Do you like ice cream?"

As she strode into the Hollingsworths' circular driveway early the next morning, Susan was pensive, thinking about the first day of work ahead of her. She was glad that she would have a chance to get to know little Nicole better. And trying to convince Michelle that the two of them could be friends, rather than adversaries, was certainly going to be a challenge. Of course, even being inside the Hollingsworths' grand house, however gloomy it still might have felt to her, would be a sort of adventure.

Yes, she definitely had a lot on her mind. Yet as she approached the front door, she was drawn out of her deep concentration. She suddenly had an uneasy feeling—the feeling that someone was watching her. She whirled around, expecting to see someone standing behind her in the driveway, or perhaps in the patch of garden or the clump of trees beyond.

But no one was there.

You're probably just imagining things, she told herself. First-day-of-work jitters, that's all. Or maybe the gardener was back there, or . . . or someone out walking a dog. . . .

She resolved to put the whole incident out of her mind. Todd was right; she *was* beginning to let her imagination run away with her.

Besides, she had much more important things to think about—like the kind of impression she was about to make this morning, on the first day of her new position as a mother's helper. She smoothed the dark purple paisley skirt she was wearing with a sleeveless white eyelet blouse, pushed a stray strand of chestnut-brown hair behind her ear, and knocked on the door with what she hoped sounded like confidence.

This time when the frowning butler came to the door, Susan wasn't at all surprised. And she was determined not to let even his sour disposition get in her way.

"Good morning!" she greeted him brightly. "And how are you on this fine morning? I'm Susan Pratt, remember? And your name is . . . ?"

The butler hesitated. It was clear that he was not used to being spoken to in such an informal manner. And it was equally clear that he didn't like it very much.

"My name is Mr. Powell," he said, pronouncing each word slowly and carefully, his English accent thick and precise. "Please come this way. Ms. Hollingsworth is expecting you."

Susan nodded and, with a spring to her step, followed Mr. Powell down the long corridor. This time she made a point of looking around more carefully. She was struck by something she hadn't really noticed the first time: a row of portraits that hung alongside the elegant staircase in the front hall.

"Excuse me, Mr. Powell," she said. "I can't help noticing all those portraits. Who are those people, exactly?"

Mr. Powell glanced up at the half dozen paintings lining the wall. For a moment a peculiar look flashed across his face. But then he regained his composure.

"Those are members of the Hollingsworth family," he replied. He hesitated, as if thinking, then added, "That is, most of them are."

After that it seemed as if his step quickened. Susan practically had to run to keep up with him. But even as she followed him into the drawing room, where she could see Ms. Hollingsworth sitting on that same chair, waiting for her, her mind was on those portraits—and Mr. Powell's odd reaction to them. She made a mental note to try to find out more about them—when the time and place were right, of course.

"Good morning, Miss Pratt—Susan," Ms. Hollingsworth greeted her. Once again there was not even a trace of a smile on her face as she extended her hand. "I am pleased that you have arrived on time. Promptness is a very important trait, especially in a young person like you."

Susan just smiled politely. Somehow, being in Ms. Hollingsworth's presence banished every bit of confidence she had.

"Before I take you upstairs to the girls' room, I would like to take you on a tour of the house. After all, for the next few weeks you will be spending a great deal of time here."

"Oh, but it's summer!" Susan protested without thinking. "I plan to take Nicole and Michelle outside as much as possible! Why, I bet they love the beach and the pool and the playgrounds! And we can always go to the Seagull Ice Cream Emporium in town. And then, in just a few days, there's that big Fourth of July celebration—"

"No!" Ms. Hollingsworth cried with more emotion than Susan had ever seen her show before. The woman

47

blinked, then regained her control. "Susan, it is very important that Michelle and Nicole be kept away from . . . that sort of thing. Their father and I are very careful about how the girls spend their time, and we are quite watchful about the kinds of things they are exposed to. I do not feel that any of those are appropriate ways for the girls to spend their time."

Susan was about to ask what *was* considered an "appropriate" way for two little girls to spend their time, if playing in the sand at the seashore and eating ice cream and watching fireworks weren't, but she realized that Ms. Hollingsworth would no doubt make that clear soon enough.

The tour of the Hollingsworths' immense house was surprisingly brief. Susan suspected that she was being shown only the rooms that she would be permitted to bring the girls into: the library, the music room, the dining room. Still, she couldn't help being awestruck as she saw more and more of the mansion, with its huge rooms, each decorated with beautiful antique and heavy fabrics, each gloomier than the rest. She noticed that there were no windows open, as if somehow the Hollingsworths wanted to keep the rest of the world *out*.

"Now," Ms. Hollingsworth said after they'd returned to the front stairway once again, "I will take you up to the girls' room and brief you on the daily schedule they are to follow—"

"Wait a minute," Susan interrupted, once again so caught up in what she was seeing that she forgot to keep her questions in check. She had just noticed another long corridor, which led to what looked like another part of the house, one that wasn't even visible from the front. "What's down here? It looks like this wing leads to the back of the house. . . . Are the girls allowed to play back there?"

When Ms. Hollingsworth didn't reply right away, Susan glanced over at her. The expression on the woman's face was one of fury. Her lips were drawn into a tight straight line, and her eyes were ablaze with anger.

"Miss Pratt," she hissed, "you are never, *never* to go into that wing of the house. Do you hear me? If I ever even *suspect* that you have trespassed in that area, I will fire you immediately. Do you understand me?"

Susan gulped. "Y-yes, Ms. Hollingsworth!" She could barely get the words out.

She was relieved when they finally reached the girls' room. They were standing almost at attention, dressed in crisp white blouses and navy-blue shirts that looked more like uniforms than the kind of clothes little girls would be wearing on a warm summer day. Nicole smiled shyly when she saw Susan. Michelle, however, made a point of not even looking over in her direction.

Ms. Hollingsworth, meanwhile, greeted the girls formally, then began to recite to Susan the daily schedule the girls were to follow.

"When you first arrive, I would like you to take the girls for a short walk around the house and the grounds, for exercise. Just make sure you stay within the areas I have outlined for you, Miss Pratt." She cast Susan a meaningful look. "And make sure their clothes remain clean. Then, from nine-thirty until ten-thirty, the girls practice the piano, downstairs in the music room. Then there will be a period of reading and studying until lunch. After lunch there will be a rest period."

"But when do the girls *play*?"

As soon as she asked the question, Susan noticed that Michelle looked horrified. But Nicole's entire face lit up, as if someone had just given her some wonderful present.

"Mr. Hollingsworth and I do not consider mindless 'play' a worthwhile way for young women to spend their time," Ms. Hollingsworth replied coldly. "We do allow what we call a recreational period, however, an hour in the afternoon. During this time you are to encourage the use of educational materials, such as maps, flash cards, art supplies—"

"Art supplies!" Susan's optimism had suddenly returned. "Now, *that's* something I can help with! As a matter of fact, I'm going to art school in the fall!"

"Art school!" Nicole cried. "How exciting—!"

"Nicole!" Ms. Hollingsworth's tone made it clear that seven-year-old girls were not expected to contribute to adult conversation. Susan watched Nicole's face fall, as if she were folding up inside like a little flower trying to protect itself from the rain.

But the little girl's natural cheerfulness was not that easy to crush. The moment Ms. Hollingsworth had left the room, Nicole came running over to Susan and threw her arms around her.

"Ooh, I'm *so* glad you're going to be our baby-sitter!" she cried. "You're so . . . so *nice*!"

Susan laughed. "I think you're nice, too, Nicole. And I have a feeling that over the next few weeks you and I are going to become great friends." She looked

50

over at Michelle and said, "And I hope you and I can be friends, too, Michelle."

Michelle just strutted over to the door. "It's only nine o'clock," she said. "We will have a half hour left for exercise."

"Oh, goody!" Nicole exclaimed. "Let's show Susan our house!" Suddenly the little girl froze, and a look of terror crossed her face. "I'm supposed to call you Miss Pratt, aren't I? I'm sorry! I'm sorry! I just forgot!"

"It's all right, Nicole!" Susan was quick to reassure her. "You can call me Susan. In fact, I *want* you to call me Susan!"

Once the little girl was certain that she hadn't done anything wrong after all, she smiled again. She took Susan's hand in her own and led her out the door. "I like you," she said, her voice nearly a whisper. "I like you a lot."

The girls' "walk" retraced much of what Susan had already seen. Even so, it was much more interesting this time around, with Nicole gleefully pointing out her favorite statue, one of a pony, an antique pitcher hand-painted with pretty roses, a needlepoint footstool that she loved to sit on. Michelle hung back, still not ready to accept Susan or, it appeared, to be part of anything that might turn out to be fun. Susan felt bad for the little girl but was quickly growing more determined than ever to win Michelle over.

And then the threesome turned a corner and found themselves back at the big staircase—the one lined with the portraits.

"Gee, look at these," Susan said casually after glancing around to make sure that Mr. Powell was

51

nowhere around. "I didn't notice these before. Aren't they grand! All these serious-looking people . . . Who are these people, Nicole?"

"This is my grandfather," Nicole said, proud that she had some information she could pass on to her new friend. "And this is *his* father, and this is some great-aunt or something. . . ."

"What about this one?" Susan gestured toward the largest one, which looked like a family portrait of four people, two men and two women, all of them in their twenties.

"That's our father."

Susan turned around, shocked that Michelle was the one who had answered her question. Sure enough, the nine-year-old was standing in front of the painting, gazing up at the faces of the four people sitting together. The one on the end, whom she had just identified as her father, looked very serious, as did the woman next to him—whom Susan now recognized as Ms. Hollingsworth when she had been a bit younger.

"And that's our aunt," Michelle went on.

"I see," said Susan.

So Ms. Hollingsworth *wasn't* the girls' mother! Her intuition on that one had been correct. It seemed that she was Mr. Hollingsworth's sister. But in that case, where *was* their mother?

"But who are these other two people?" Susan looked at them more carefully and saw that this man and woman, unlike anyone else in any of the other portraits, were *smiling*. In fact, they both looked like friendly, likable people. The man was rather handsome. As for the woman, she was strikingly beautiful, with clear blue eyes, thick dark hair, and a playful tilt to her chin. But as Susan turned to Michelle, she saw that the little girl was looking at them with anger in her eyes.

"That's my other aunt. She died a long time ago, even before we moved here, to Seagull Island."

"Oh, I'm sorry to hear that. And who's the man next to her?"

"That's our uncle. He was bad." Michelle spat out her words. "He was very bad. In fact, he was so bad that he's not allowed to come see us anymore, not ever again."

Susan was startled by Michelle's tone of voice. The girl sounded as if she hated that man. And yet Susan couldn't imagine what terrible thing he had done to warrant a little girl's hatred. . . .

Just then a huge clock somewhere in the house resounded with a loud bong.

"It's nine-thirty!" Nicole gasped. "We have to get to the music room right away! It's time for us to practice the piano." She slipped her hand into Susan's and started to lead her away.

Michelle, meanwhile, stayed behind, staring at the portrait. Susan was surprised, but she left the girl alone, instead letting Nicole lead her down the hall.

"Do you know what?" the younger girl whispered as soon as they were far enough away from the pensive Michelle that she wasn't likely to overhear what they were saying.

"No, Nicole. What?"

"I *remember* our uncle. You know, the one Michelle was talking about. . . . The one she said was so bad. I was just a teensy little girl when he used to come here, but I remember him. I'm sure I do!"

"I believe you," Susan replied kindly. "Tell me, Nicole. What did your uncle do to make everyone hate him so much, so much that he's not even allowed to come into this house anymore?"

Susan looked over at Nicole and saw that her eyes had filled with tears. "I don't know!" Nicole whispered. "And do you know what else? I don't hate him, not at all! I remember him as being a very nice man! I remember him bringing me toys and telling me stories and . . . and I'm not sure, but I think he brought us a puppy once, but we weren't allowed to keep it—"

"Miss Pratt! Are you aware that it is nine-thirty?" Ms. Hollingsworth's sharp voice snapped Susan back to the moment. "It is time for the girls' music hour."

"Yes, Ms. Hollingsworth. Nicole and I were just on our way to the music room. Michelle is right behind me. . . ."

For the next hour, Susan sat in the elegant music room, with its huge windows overlooking the garden and not one but two grand pianos, on which the girls took turns practicing their music lessons. But it wasn't the pretty Mozart sonatas that Susan was thinking about as she sat there, daydreaming.

It was Michelle and Nicole's mysterious "uncle," this man whom Michelle said she hated and Nicole said she had once liked. Like so many other things that went on at the Hollingsworths' house, it just didn't make any sense.

I don't care what anyone says, Susan thought as Nicole's little fingers flew over the piano keys, playing a beautiful melody that reflected how much time and discipline she had already put into her music even at such a young age. There's definitely something strange going on around here. And I intend to get to the bottom of it, no matter what it takes.

Even if I have to sneak into the wing of the house that Ms. Hollingsworth forbade me to go into. . . .

And then, even though it was a warm day and the windows in the music room were tightly shut against any hint of the breeze that might have been in the air, Susan shivered.

Six

"This is practically a dream come true!" joked Chris with a grin. "Imagine: for the next few weeks I'll actually be *paid* to spend my days surrounded by a dozen wonderful flavors of homemade ice cream, with an open invitation from the Coopers themselves to help myself to as much as I want! Why, this scoop is more like a magic wand than a simple tool of the trade!"

In order to demonstrate her first-day-of-work enthusiasm, Chris dramatically waved her ice-cream scoop over the Seagull Ice Cream Emporium's glass-covered display case, in which there were twelve five-gallon drums of freshly made ice cream.

Neil laughed. "And we're not just talking your basic vanilla, chocolate, and strawberry here, either. We've got chocolate almond chip and mocha fudge and peach parfait. . . ."

"And I intend to taste every single one of them, every single day!" With mock seriousness Chris added, "to make sure that their quality is up to the Coopers' usual high standards, of course! After all, it's part of our job to make sure that this place remains popular."

"Well, I'm pretty sure we won't have any trouble in that department," said Neil with a chuckle. "Today is only your first day, but you'll see soon enough that there's a steady stream of people coming into this place. Sure, business is a little bit lighter than it was last year or even the year before. But even so, we'll be busy enough. There'll be people spending the day sunning themselves at the beach, people coming into town to do some shopping, even people who are just out for a stroll. Maybe the tourist trade is down compared to other years, but sooner or later just about everybody who lives on Seagull Island comes into the Seagull Ice Cream Emporium."

"I'm beginning to see what you mean!"

Not two minutes had passed since Chris had turned over the red and black cardboard sign on the glass front door, changing its message from Closed to Open, yet already the first customers of the day were coming inside. She took her place at the take-out counter, leaving the more complicated ice cream treats, like sundaes and sodas and banana splits, to her more experienced coworker.

Their first customer was a young couple, vacationing on the island, who couldn't resist indulging in chocolate sodas, even though it was still late morning. Then came a woman who needed a quart of vanilla for a small dinner party she was holding that evening. Next, two small boys who had apparently been saving their pennies and nickels for weeks in order to splurge on butterscotch sundaes the moment they had come up

57

with enough money. Chris noticed that Neil was extra generous as he scooped up their ice cream.

One by one the customers came, sometimes so many at one time that a small line formed. Chris lost count of them . . . and she lost track of the time. When she finally took a moment to stop to catch her breath and look at the clock, she gasped.

"My goodness! It's already past three! Where has the day gone?"

"Time flies when you're working hard, doesn't it?" Neil teased. "But this is always a slow time of day. How about taking a break? Didn't you bring your lunch with you today?"

Chris eyed the brown paper bag she had tucked under the counter, in which she had packed a sandwich and an apple. Suddenly, eating something *other* than ice cream sounded appetizing indeed.

"I never thought I'd see the day," she joked to Neil as she took a seat at the counter, "but after spending four hours serving ice cream to other people, I'd actually *prefer* eating something else!"

No sooner had she bit into her sandwich than she heard another customer come into the store. She started to stand up, ready to return to her place at the take-out counter, when Neil said, "That's okay, Chris. I'll handle this one."

She turned and saw that the man who had just come in was quite a bit different from all the vacationers and townspeople who had been patronizing the Seagull Ice Cream Emporium all day. It was clear from the well-worn clothes he was wearing that he had fallen on hard times. His brown hair was in need of cutting, and he could have used a shave. Even more than that, however, there was an air of defeat about him somehow, a look of sadness in his clear blue eyes, an expression of woefulness on what Chris could see was really a very nice-looking face. She was immediately overcome by feelings of sympathy for this man, and she found herself wondering if there was any way in which she could help him.

But Neil, she quickly saw, had already taken the matter into his hands.

"Hey, Happy Jack!" he greeted the man with a warm, welcoming smile. "Come on in! What'll it be today?"

"Ah, nothing for me," the man replied, sidling up to the counter and sitting down on one of the stools. "Just came in to say hello."

"Oh, too bad," Neil replied. "Because I was hoping you'd do me a favor and help me get rid of some of these extra bananas we got stuck with. For some reason, the Coopers' supplier sent over a couple of extra bunches, more than we could ever use, even if everybody on the entire island suddenly decided they just had to have banana splits." From behind the counter, Neil brought out two huge bunches of bananas. "I'd really hate it if we just had to let these go to waste. . . ."

"Well, in that case . . ."

The man—"Happy Jack," as Neil had called him with such cheerful familiarity—hesitated for a moment, then reached over and took the bananas.

"Thanks, Neil," he said in a voice hoarse with gratitude. "Thanks a lot."

As soon as the man had left, just a few minutes after he'd sauntered into the store, Chris looked over at Neil and demanded, "Neil Weaver, what on earth was that all about? You know full well we didn't get more bananas than we needed!"

"I know that," Neil said thoughtfully. "And to tell you the truth, I'm pretty sure that Happy Jack knows that, too. But, well, that man is kind of an institution around here. Everybody in town does whatever they can to help him out. He's had some hard luck, as you can see, and people like Mr. Cooper are always ready to give him a hand whenever they can."

"Who exactly is he? Does he have a job? Has he always lived here on Seagull Island?"

Neil thought for a few seconds. "There's a lot I don't know about the man, Chris. He's kind of mysterious, if you know what I mean. He doesn't have much money; he works doing odd jobs for people, mostly around people's summer homes. He lives in a little house—a shack, really—by the sea. It's up on the beach about a mile from here, away from everybody else. He's a nice man . . . but one who seems to have a secret past."

"It's too bad," said Chris. "He seems nice . . . and a little sad."

Before she had a chance to think about poor Happy Jack, however, a few more customers came in. Chris wolfed down the rest of her sandwich, tucked her apple in her pocket, and took her place at the take-out counter, forgetting all about Happy Jack for the moment.

ANOTHER CHEMICAL DUMP! the headlines of Thursday morning's *Seagull Island Gazette* screamed.

"Oh, dear," Rosemary Stevens said with a sigh as she glanced at the front page over breakfast, having just picked the newspaper up off the front porch, where it was delivered every week. "More bad news, I'm afraid."

"Let me see that." Susan frowned as her grandmother handed her the paper, and she, too, read the headlines. "This is terrible! There's been *another* illegal dumping of chemicals into Seagull Harbor!"

"Oh, no!" Chris groaned. "There goes any chance I ever had of trying out that wonderful ocean!"

"You . . . and a few thousand tourists," said Bill Stevens. "I bet there are a lot of businesspeople around here who are very upset this morning. And your friends the Coopers are among them, no doubt."

"It's true that business over at the Seagull Ice Cream Emporium is slower than it has been in other years," Chris admitted. "At least, according to what Neil's noticed."

"What I want to know is, what's being *done* about it?"

Bill, Rosemary, and Chris all turned to look at Susan, whose vehemence had caught them by surprise. She had skimmed the article quickly as the others were talking and had learned that there was not yet a single clue as to who was responsible—or who would pay for a cleanup.

"I mean, this is really an awful thing!" Susan went on. "Some company is polluting the waters of Seagull Harbor, using areas that are supposed to be reserved for recreational use as . . . as *garbage pails*, just because it's cheaper and easier than arranging to have its chemical waste disposed of properly—"

"Hold on, Sooz!" her sister interrupted with a teasing chuckle. "You sound as if you're about to embark on a one-woman crusade!"

"Well . . . maybe I am," Susan said lamely, feeling her cheeks grow pink.

"That's a very noble sentiment," said the twins' grandmother. "And I think it's important for all of us to be concerned—and involved. But I'm afraid that this is something that's entirely out of our control."

"According to what I'm reading in this article," interjected Bill Stevens, "it's even out of the control of the local political officials. Not to mention this investigative reporter—now, what's his name? Here it is. Adam Price. Yes, as I recall, he wrote the other articles about this same subject last week, when the first chemical dumping took place."

"But don't you agree that—"

"Come on, Sooz." Chris jabbed her twin sister in the ribs playfully, then reached across the table for a second cinnamon bun. "I know that you and I have built up quite a reputation as sleuths, what with the way we're always going around, sticking our noses into other people's business. But what do you say that for a change we let it go? We deserve the summer off!"

Susan opened her mouth to protest but instead just let out a loud sigh. "Sure," she said. "I guess you're right." But it was only too clear that her agreement was reluctant. She had decided not to belabor the point, having concluded that since her grandparents and her sister all felt that there was nothing that any of them could do, it was best just to let the subject drop.

But just because I've decided not to *talk* about it, thought Susan as she joined the others' discussion of the Stevenses' growing skill as golfers, doesn't mean that I intend to stop *thinking* about it!

* * *

"What a week!" With a loud groan Chris flopped across her bed, without even giving a second thought to the possibility of wrinkling the red and white striped shirt and the pair of navy-blue shorts she had made a point of wearing this evening. "And to think that a mere five days ago I actually believed that it was going to be *fun* working at an ice-cream parlor!"

Her twin sister, standing in front of the mirror that hung above the girls' dresser, glanced over with an amused smile. "Christine Pratt, do you mean to tell me that *you*, of all people, have finally become sick of ice cream?"

"Oh, no! It's nothing like that! I still love eating it! No, the thing that came as such a surprise to me is that scooping ice cream all day is *hard work*!"

To demonstrate, she sat up abruptly, made a fist, and held out her right arm, bent at the elbow, the muscles flexed. "Just look at those biceps, Sooz! And check out those triceps!"

Susan couldn't help laughing. "Well, look at it this way, Chris. By the end of the summer you'll be an even stronger swimmer than you ever were before."

"I suppose that's true." With a sigh, Chris retrieved her hairbrush from the small wooden table next to her bed and joined her sister at the mirror. "This is no time to be thinking about work, anyway. Not when our first full weekend on Seagull Island is about to begin."

"And what a weekend! Fourth of July weekend is always chock-full of excitement, no matter where you are."

"And Seagull Island is certainly one place that's pulling out all the stops!" Chris said heartily. "An outdoor band concert and fireworks display tonight, the big parade tomorrow, the community cookout on

Sunday . . . It's going to be impossible for us *not* to have a good time!"

Chris looked over at her sister's reflection in the mirror, expecting her to be nodding in agreement. Instead, she was surprised to see that Susan's expression was serious—almost glum.

"What on earth is *wrong*, Sooz?"

"Oh, I was just thinking." Slowly she pulled her hairbrush through her chestnut-brown locks, then added, "I was thinking about Michelle and Nicole."

"Really? What about them?"

"Well, here this huge Fourth of July celebration is about to begin, three whole days full of fun that are meant for everyone on Seagull Island to enjoy. . . . And those poor little girls aren't going to be allowed to participate in *any* of it."

Chris looked astonished. She set her hairbrush down on the dresser and turned to face her sister. "What are you talking about, Sooz? Why aren't they?"

Susan sighed. "I guess you and I have both been so busy this week, working hard at our new jobs all day and then falling into bed early, that we really haven't had a chance to talk about what we've been doing, have we? And now we don't have much time either, since we're supposed to be meeting Neil and Todd in a few minutes. . . ."

"Neil and Todd can wait." Wearing an earnest expression, Chris plopped down on the edge of the bed. "Okay, Sooz. Let's have it. I want to hear every single detail about your new job and these two little girls you're taking care of—and I *especially* want to know why a seven-year-old and her nine-year-old sister aren't allowed to go to a Fourth of July concert and fireworks display!"

It didn't take long for Susan to tell her sister about all the peculiar things she had been noticing at the Hollingsworths' house ever since the day of her job interview, five days earlier. Chris listened intently, her face drawn into a pensive frown, as Susan talked about the strict way in which the girls were being raised; their sour-faced aunt, who had somehow been permitted to take charge of their lives; the wing of the somber Victorian house that was closed off to her; the eerie feeling she often got as she was entering or leaving the house, the feeling that she was being watched. She finished up by telling Chris about the mysterious "uncle" who had disappeared, a man whom Michelle remembered as being a terrible person but of whom Nicole had only fond memories.

"Wow!" Chris breathed when she had finished. "You were right, Sooz! There *is* a lot of funny stuff going on in that big, creepy house!" Her brown eyes grew big and round as she added, "And I'll bet you're just itching to get to the bottom of it all!"

Susan grinned ruefully. "Well, to tell you the truth, Chris, it did occur to me once or twice that it might be interesting to find out what the Hollingsworths' secrets are all about. But I don't see how. Especially since I have a feeling that the wing of the house that Ms. Hollingsworth made sure to tell me was off-limits has something to do with all the mystery around that place. . . ."

"Hey, there! Anybody up for a ride into town?"

Their grandfather's hearty voice interrupted their discussion. The twins glanced up, surprised, having forgotten all about their plans for the evening until that very moment.

"Goodness! What time is it?" Susan looked at her watch and then cried, "Oh, no! We're supposed to meet Todd and Neil in only seven minutes!"

"In that case, Grandpa, we'd love a ride into town. Are you and Grandma going to the outdoor concert?"

"Wouldn't miss it! In fact, Grandma's already backing the car out of the driveway. Hop in, and we'll have you girls at the band shell in no time!"

Sure enough, Susan and Chris arrived just in time at the spot that had been designated as the meeting place for the twins and their dates for the evening. And the expressions on the boys' faces told them right away that there was one significant fact Susan and Chris had each neglected to mention over the week or so since they had met.

"There are *two* of you!" Todd exclaimed.

Neil just burst out laughing. "Well, I never . . . !"

"Oops!" Chris grinned. "I guess that when I told you my sister would be coming along tonight, I didn't say anything about the fact that the two of us are identical twins."

"Nope. That's one fact you left out!"

But there was little time for the boys to dwell on their astonishment. The concert was scheduled to begin in only a few minutes, and the foursome was anxious to get a good place on the huge grounds surrounding the band shell.

No sooner had they spread out their blanket and gotten comfortable, looking forward to an evening of music and fireworks under the stars, than Susan let out a loud gasp.

"Oh, my gosh!" she cried, clapping her hand over her mouth.

"What is it, Sooz?" Puzzled, Chris looked over in the direction in which her twin was staring, eyes wide with surprise. All she saw was a row of high bushes lining the edge of the huge green lawn, which tonight was covered with Seagull Islanders and summer visitors, all ready for the evening's entertainment.

"Chris, I know this sounds crazy, but I could swear I just saw . . ."

"What? Who? Sooz, what on earth is going on?"

"I thought I just saw Michelle and Nicole. And someone else with them, someone with bright red hair. . . ."

"But that's impossible! You told me not thirty minutes ago that Ms. Hollingsworth made a point of telling you that they weren't allowed to come to any of the Fourth of July festivities. . . ." Chris peered in the direction of the bushes, trying to see something. But she saw nothing—only greenery. "Are you *sure*, Sooz?"

"Well, no. I guess I just imagined it." Susan laughed self-consciously. "Maybe I'm starting to see things. No doubt the result of spending too much time worrying about the Hollingsworths."

"Or maybe it's the excitement of the holiday weekend," Chris suggested. "Besides, it *is* starting to get kind of dark."

Just as Susan had decided that it all must have been a mistake and that the best thing for her to do was forget all about it and sit back and enjoy the concert, the musicians began to file into the band shell and take their places. But when the bandleader came out and stepped up onto the platform at the edge of the stage, he turned to face the audience and raised his arms for silence.

"Good evening, ladies and gentlemen," he boomed. "Welcome to tonight's Fourth of July concert, an event that marks the beginning of an entire weekend of holiday festivities. I hope you'll take part in them—and enjoy yourselves. Tonight, before our performance gets under way, I am pleased to introduce our most honored guest for the evening: Mayor Thomas Jackson!"

There was a round of applause as a dignified-looking man came onto the stage, one of the few men wearing a suit and tie this evening.

"Good evening, and welcome!" the mayor said. "Tonight is a time of celebration . . . but as both the citizens of Seagull Island and our summertime guests know, we are currently facing a crisis, one that threatens not only the island's economy but our environment as well. I've invited a good friend of mine here to speak to you briefly about the situation. I am pleased and proud to introduce one of Seagull Island's most concerned citizens: Mr. Charles Hollingsworth!"

Susan gasped. "That's *him*!" she cried, tugging on her sister's arm. "Michelle and Nicole's father! The one who won't let them go anywhere or do anything . . . and the one who Todd says is such an upstanding citizen!"

"Let's hear what he has to say." Chris sat up straight, her eyes fixed on the stage. A good-looking man, also dressed in a suit and tie, strode confidently onto the stage and shook hands with Mayor Jackson.

"A terrible thing has happened here on Seagull Island," Charles Hollingsworth began once things had quieted down again. "As I'm sure most of you know, someone—a company, an individual, a group of individuals—has been dumping thousands of gallons of chemical pollutants into our waters. As yet no one has been able to get to the bottom of it. But as your friend and neighbor, as well as a local businessman, I want to assure you that Mayor Jackson is having the matter investigated fully. In fact, he has formed a task force—of which I am the head—to find out who is responsible and to make sure that reparations are made."

Susan listened carefully as he went on, continuing to reassure everyone that the matter would soon be under control. She was fascinated not only by what he had to say but also by the man himself. After all, he was Michelle and Nicole's father—someone she had never actually met but someone in whom she had been quite interested, right from the start. The strict manner in which the little girls were being raised was no doubt *his* doing, as well as Marion Hollingsworth's. Yet it was difficult for Susan to find any fault with this man as he spoke confidently from the stage, persuading the entire audience that the situation of the dangerous and illegal chemical dumping was going to be taken care of.

As he concluded his speech and the band members picked up their instruments, Susan, like the others in the audience, was confident that Charles Hollingsworth would manage to solve the problem of the chemical dumping. It was almost a relief to be able to put it out of her mind.

She leaned back and got comfortable, reminding herself that it was time for her to start enjoying herself, to forget all her worries and concerns. It was a beautiful Friday evening, the concert was about to begin, and she was sitting beside a very nice boy whom she was already starting to like very much.

It's my summer vacation, and from now on I'm going to concentrate on having *fun*! she decided with great determination. I'm going to forget all about both the Hollingsworths *and* Seagull Harbor's pollution problems!

Little did Susan know as she sat under the stars, listening to the stirring introduction to a famous Sousa march, that exactly one week from this very night she would be deeply involved in a dangerous scheme designed to solve the mysteries of both.

Seven

The fun and excitement of the festive Fourth of July weekend—as well as Susan's resolution to let Charles Hollingsworth do all the worrying about both his family and the pollution of Seagull Harbor—was all forgotten the moment Susan stepped into the Hollingsworths' house, ready to begin her second week of working there. The tension within the household was so thick that she knew, without even needing to ask, that something had happened.

"Good morning, Susan," Marion Hollingsworth greeted her crisply, sounding even more formal than usual. "Even though this household is in an uproar, the girls are upstairs in their bedroom as usual, waiting for you."

Stifling the urge to ask what was going on, Susan just nodded and started up the stairs. But she stopped as she felt Ms. Hollingsworth's hand clamp around her arm.

"Just a minute, Susan. There are some additional instructions this morning."

"Yes?" As Susan looked into Ms. Hollingsworth's dark brown eyes this morning, she was struck, as always, by the lack of friendliness or compassion reflected in them.

"Until further notice, Nicole and Michelle are not to leave this house. Do you understand?"

"Not even to go into their own backyard—?"

"Miss Pratt," the frowning woman snapped, her eyes growing narrow, "you have always seemed to me to be an intelligent and responsible young woman. I trust you know what I mean when I say that the girls are *not to leave this house*! Not to go into the yard, not to go anywhere. And that rule, I might add, will stand until further notice."

"All right," Susan said quietly. "But I do have one question. What would you like the girls to do in place of their usual morning outing?"

Ms. Hollingsworth thought for a moment. Obviously, she hadn't considered this before. And then she said, "Take them upstairs, into the solarium."

"The solarium?"

"Yes. Surely you've heard of a solarium. In case you haven't, it's a room with glass walls, designed to let in as much sun as possible. . . ."

"I know what a solarium is. But where is it?" Susan was confused. "I don't remember having seen any place like that."

Ms. Hollingsworth hesitated before answering. "It's on the third floor, where the back wing joins the main part of the house."

Susan just nodded, not letting on for even a second that the very *idea* of getting so close to the "forbidden wing" of the Hollingsworths' house was making her heart pound like a jackhammer.

It was all she could do to contain her excitement as she burst into the girls' bedroom. She found them waiting for her, just the same as on every other morning. And, just as on other mornings, Nicole greeted her with a big hug and an enthusiastic "Susan! I'm so glad you're here!" while Michelle barely acknowledged her arrival at all.

"You'll *never* guess what happened!" Nicole cried, her blue eyes big and round as she took Susan by the hand and led her over to the corner of the room in which she kept all her favorite toys. "Something *terrible* . . . at least it must be, by the way everyone's been acting all morning. You should have seen my father and my aunt this morning, over breakfast. Why, they were both so furious that neither of them ate a thing!"

"Nicole, what happened?" asked Susan.

"Somebody broke into the house and stole a beautiful antique jeweled box from the front parlor!"

"Wait a minute. When did this happen, Nicole? And if somebody actually got inside this house, why did they steal a *box* . . . but nothing else?"

"I don't know." Nicole's mouth drooped into a pensive pout as she pondered all that she *didn't* know about this somewhat strange occurrence that had upset the entire household so. "But I *do* know that the box that's missing belonged to my grandmother once. But then she gave it to my mother as a wedding present. It was a beautiful box. It was probably very valuable, too. It was gold, with rubies and emeralds and sapphires."

Once again Susan found herself bewildered by the

mysteries of the Hollingsworth household—and unable to resist being intrigued by them. She was on the verge of asking some of the many questions she had about the mysterious Hollingsworth family—like who the girls' real mother was, and where she was now, and how their dreadful Aunt Marion had ever come to rule their lives with such a cold, unfeeling hand. But when she saw the sadness that had clouded the little girl's eyes, she decided it was best not to press Nicole any further.

Before Susan had a chance to say anything consoling, Michelle suddenly interrupted.

"Daddy says he knows *exactly* who stole that box! And he's pretty mad about it, too. If that evil man even *thinks* he's going to get away with something like that—"

"*What* evil man?" Susan demanded. "Michelle, how does your father know for sure who stole that box? And *why* did he take it—one jeweled box and nothing else? Who would do something like that?"

But Michelle didn't seem to have heard anything that Susan had said. Instead, the nine-year-old girl's eyes narrowed angrily.

"And I bet that it's no coincidence that this happened *now*, right before the big fund-raising party!"

"*What* big fund-raising party?"

Michelle looked over at Susan and blinked in surprise, as if she expected that *everyone* would know what she was referring to. "Why, the Hollingsworths' annual fund-raising party. Every year, the weekend after the Fourth of July, our family has a big party to raise money for charity. Then we donate the money to whoever we decide deserves it the most."

"You mean, whoever *needs* it the most," Michelle's younger sister corrected her gently.

Susan smiled. How different these two sisters were! And, as always, she couldn't help wondering how they had ever turned out so unalike, what different forces there could have been in their early lives that had shaped them into the kinds of people they were now.

She turned to Nicole. "Nicole, do you know who your father thinks took that box?"

The little girl shook her head seriously. "No."

"Michelle, you seem to think that you know. Who was it?"

But Michelle just shrugged, muttered, "Hmph!" and turned away.

At this point Susan decided that the best thing to do was change the subject. Even so, she was wondering if perhaps by being just a little bit clever she could manage to find some more clues to the seemingly endless stream of secrets that this family was guarding.

"So," she said, trying to keep her voice casual, "did you two have fun celebrating the Fourth of July?"

As soon as she'd asked the question, she noticed that Nicole and Michelle exchanged nervous glances. But she pretended she hadn't seen a thing.

"On Friday night Daddy had to give an important speech," Nicole finally said. "Then on Saturday night Daddy made charcoal-broiled steaks outside in the backyard, and we sat outside and had lemonade and corn on the cob for dinner."

"That sounds like fun!" Susan said brightly.

"Well . . ." Nicole hesitated. "I suppose it might have been fun, but Aunt Marion told us to wear our white dresses, and then she got really mad at us for getting them dirty. We weren't allowed to have any dessert."

Susan's mouth dropped open—but she remembered just in time that it wasn't right for her to say anything about the way Ms. Hollingsworth was raising her two nieces.

But that doesn't keep me from having my own feelings about it! she thought angrily. What a mean woman she is. . . . And what kind of father is Charles Hollingsworth, for allowing it all to happen? Imagine, making the girls wear white dresses that were *bound* to get soiled at an outdoor barbecue, then punishing them on what was supposed to be a holiday celebration and no doubt ruining the whole evening. . . . Oh, it's just not fair!

Then she remembered something else that hadn't been fair: the fact that Nicole and Michelle hadn't been allowed to attend any of Seagull Island's varied July Fourth festivities.

"Well, I had a good time," Susan reported. "Friday night I heard your father give his speech. I went to an outdoor band concert, and at the end there was a fireworks display that was magnificent!"

"Oh, wasn't it wonderful?" As soon as the words had slipped out, Nicole clapped her hand over her mouth. "I mean, we saw it through the window. Didn't we, Michelle? We leaned out the window, this one, right here. . . ."

Michelle nodded. "That's right," she said, her chin held at an angle that defied anyone to disagree with her. "We saw the fireworks through this window."

Susan suspected that the girls weren't telling the

truth, but since they were unwilling to confide in her, she couldn't be certain.

Maybe I did see them out at the band shell . . . or maybe I just imagined it, she thought. They probably could have seen the fireworks from here. Besides, there was that woman with the red hair that I also saw, and I know for a fact that there's no one in this house who has red hair! And with these girls as isolated as they are, I doubt that there's anyone else who'd be in a position to sneak them out. . . .

No, I must have been mistaken. Either I imagined the whole thing, or I saw two little girls who looked kind of like Nicole and Michelle from far away.

Still, the whole episode was something she couldn't put to rest quite as easily as she would have liked.

But there was no time to dwell on it. Before long it was time for the girls' morning "walk"—today, of course, to be substituted with a stroll up to the third floor, to the solarium. The threesome made their way upstairs, being careful to act particularly somber, in light of the general mood of the house.

The solarium was a wonderful place. It was a large, sunny room filled with healthy plants and comfortable padded furniture. What was most surprising about it, however, was the fact that Ms. Hollingsworth hadn't told Susan about it earlier—that she hadn't encouraged her to take the girls there more regularly.

"What a marvelous room!" Susan exclaimed sincerely as the girls led her inside. "Why don't you ever come play here?"

"We're not allowed," Nicole replied matter-of-factly.

"Why not?"

"Because it's too close to the old, broken-down wing of the house."

Susan was confused. "What do you mean, Nicole?"

"That whole wing of the house is in terrible shape," the little girl explained patiently. "Aunt Marion says it could fall down at any minute. It's not safe for anybody to go there. No one is allowed in those rooms—*especially* little girls who can hardly stand still for a minute!"

Susan had to smile at Nicole's repetition of what were obviously the exact words that had been spoken to her. And the explanation did make perfect sense.

Well, Susan thought as she settled back in one of the soft, comfortable chairs, that solves *one* of the mysteries of the Hollingsworth mansion! The only reason that wing is off-limits to me and everybody else is that it's about to come tumbling down!

The smile that crossed her lips as she thought about how silly she had been to think there was any more to that "secret" than that, that once again she had been letting her imagination run away with her, had barely faded when some movement in the corridor outside the solarium caught her eye. She turned just in time to see what it was.

Someone had just strolled casually out of the "forbidden" wing of the house, the rooms that were supposedly on the verge of falling apart at any minute!

And as if that weren't shocking enough in itself, that "someone" was a young woman dressed in white . . . with bright red hair!

Eight

"Well, well, well!" said Neil with a chuckle. "Am I seeing double, or has the *other* Chris Pratt just walked into the Seagull Ice Cream Emporium?"

Chris hastened to set things straight as she glanced up from the glass countertop she was wiping clean with a damp cloth and saw that her twin had, indeed, just walked into the shop.

"Susan may *look* just like me—seeming as if she's, as you put it, 'the *other* Chris Pratt'—but she and I are really very different from each other."

"That's right," Susan agreed, sidling up to the counter and perching on one of the round stools in front of it. "Sure, Chris and I are identical—but only on the outside. On the inside we're as different as . . . well, as chocolate and vanilla."

"I'll say! For one thing, Susan is a wonderfully talented artist."

"And Christine here is a first-rate swimmer."

"Susan is a whiz in history. . . ."

"And Chris *always* gets an A in math. . . ."

"Whoa! Hold on a minute!" Laughing, Neil held up his hands as if in surrender. "All right, all right. I'm convinced that you two are really nothing alike, even if you *do* look like mirror images of each other! And I'll tell you what. To show you just how well I understand what you're saying, I propose a new kind of double-dip cone in your honor: a scoop of chocolate and a scoop of vanilla!"

"Sounds terrific!" Susan grew serious, however, as she watched Neil take a sugar cone off the back counter and fill it with a generous scoop of the rich homemade ice cream. "I could use something cold and refreshing. It's been a tough day."

"Michelle and Nicole running you ragged?" Chris teased. It was the end of her workday, too, and she took advantage of the fact by climbing onto a stool beside her sister, ready to play the role of customer for a change, after having waited on customers herself since eleven o'clock that morning.

She expected her twin to smile at the suggestion that handling two little girls was proving to be harder than she'd expected. But instead, Susan's expression remained somber.

"No, it's not Nicole and Michelle. They're no trouble at all. Especially Nicole. Why, it's a joy just being with her. I'm afraid it's something else entirely. Chris, remember all the things I told you the other night? Well, I've come to the conclusion that there's definitely something funny going on around the Hollingsworths' house. I keep on running into all kinds of things that simply don't make any sense."

By now Chris, too, looked serious. "Gee, Sooz. What's happened now?"

Susan told her sister and Neil all about the mysterious disappearance of the jeweled box, as well as everything else that had happened that day: Michelle's contention that she knew exactly who'd stolen it; Susan's first peek at the secret wing of the house, the wing that was, in general, "off-limits"; her unexpected sighting of a woman with red hair, very possibly the same woman whom she had spotted at the concert three nights earlier.

"Boy, Sooz," Chris said with a sigh after her sister had finished, "it *does* sound as if there's something odd going on over there."

Neil came over to where the girls were sitting. He was bearing a huge ice-cream cone for Susan and looking interested in what she'd been saying. "And it sounds as if they don't want anybody to find out what it is, either!"

"Well, I sure wish I could find out what all the mystery is about," Susan concluded. "I haven't given up on the possibility of doing that, either. After all, we've still got most of the summer ahead, and if anybody can put the pieces of this puzzle together, it's the Pratt twins!"

" 'We'?" Chris repeated, casting her twin sister a meaningful look.

Susan just smiled as she took a large lick of her ice-cream cone. "Don't tell me *you're* not curious, too, Christine Pratt!"

But before the girls had a chance to discuss Susan's growing interest in investigating the mysterious Hollingsworth household, the screen door of the Seagull Ice Cream Emporium swung open and another customer strolled in. Susan barely noticed, since she was already deeply absorbed by the flavorful ice cream she

81

was devouring, realizing for the very first time just how hungry she really was.

Chris, however, glanced over her shoulder, saw who had just come in, and immediately forgot all about the Hollingsworths and about Susan's suggestion that some sleuthing by the Pratt twins might be in order.

"Happy Jack!" she cried, her face lighting up. "Hello! How are you?"

The man's sad face brightened in response to Chris's friendly greeting.

"Hello there, young lady. Why, I don't believe we've actually met, even though I remember having seen you the last time I was in here. But I see that you already know who I am."

Chris blushed. "Well, after you left, Neil here told me that everyone on the island calls you Happy Jack."

"That's right." The man's blue eyes were shining now. He looked just as downtrodden as he had the last time Chris had seen him—and she felt just as she had the last time, that this was a kind individual who had fallen upon some difficult times. And once again she found herself wishing there were some way in which she could help him.

"My name is Christine Pratt," she went on, sliding off her stool and extending her hand.

Happy Jack smiled warmly. "I'm pleased to meet you, Chris."

"And this is my twin sister, Susan."

"Aha. I can see the resemblance!"

Susan looked up from her ice-cream cone. "Hello. I'm pleased to meet you."

Suddenly a cloud seemed to flicker across Happy Jack's face. "Your parents are very lucky to have two lovely daughters like you girls. I hope they appreciate it."

Susan and Chris exchanged puzzled glances. What an odd thing to say!

But before they had a chance to find out what their new friend meant by his strange comment, Neil interrupted.

"So, Happy Jack. What'll it be tonight? Or is this just a social call?"

"As a matter of fact, I'm here to buy myself an ice-cream cone." He looked over at the girls and winked. "A little summer treat."

"I recommend a double-dip cone," said Susan. "One scoop of chocolate and one of vanilla."

"That sounds like an excellent combination. A chocolate and vanilla cone it is!"

"You've got it!"

As Neil turned away and began scooping up the ice cream for his cone, Chris suddenly said, "Oh, gee, if everybody else is having one, I will, too. I never did have very much willpower when it came to ice cream!"

With that, she hopped off her stool and headed over to the take-out counter, her usual post. She grabbed a scoop and dug into the five-gallon container of chocolate ice cream.

"Well, now, let me just make sure I brought along enough money." Happy Jack happened to be standing right next to Susan as he reached into his pants pocket and began bringing out change. The first time he dug into his pocket, he brought out a few nickels and dimes, which he deposited on the countertop, counting under his breath. Susan was only half watching, not really paying very much attention.

That is, until he reached into his pocket the second time—and brought out a tiny jeweled box, which was shiny gold and studded with emeralds and rubies and sapphires, the greens and reds and blues so brilliant that they had to be real.

Susan nearly choked on her ice cream. She watched in horror as Happy Jack realized what he had done. A peculiar look crossed his face, and he quickly tucked it back into his pocket. Susan glanced around and saw that neither Chris nor Neil had noticed, since they were both standing with their backs toward Susan and Happy Jack. And from the way he was acting, it was apparent that he had no idea that Susan had seen, either.

But she *had* seen. And she could come to only one conclusion: Happy Jack was the person who had stolen that precious jeweled box from the Hollingsworths!

By the time Chris returned to her stool, proudly holding a huge ice-cream cone, Happy Jack had finished counting out his change, discovering, much to his satisfaction, that he did indeed have enough money for his cone.

Susan just kept staring at him. She was trying to act as if nothing were out of the ordinary, but she couldn't help looking at him. An actual *thief* was standing just a few inches away from her!

As Chris and Neil chatted away, talking to Happy Jack about the one topic that was on everyone's mind these days, the polluting of Seagull Harbor, Susan suddenly remembered Michelle's words of earlier that day.

Daddy says he knows exactly who stole that box! And he's pretty mad about it, too. If that evil man even thinks he's going to get away with something like that . . .

So the Hollingsworths *knew* that Happy Jack had stolen the jeweled box! And they believed that he was "evil."

Susan looked at the bedraggled man beside her. It was obvious from his appearance that he was poor. Was it possible that it was simply the fact that he had so little money that had prompted Michelle and her father to accuse him of breaking into their house and stealing what seemed to be a very valuable antique?

She felt sorry for him. He did seem like a nice man as he sat talking to Chris and Neil, enjoying his ice-cream cone.

And then he turned to her. With a big smile, he said, "You were right, Susan. A chocolate and vanilla cone turned out to be a very good choice."

She knew she should say something back, but suddenly she froze. Her heart seemed to have stopped beating. She just kept staring at Happy Jack, unable to move, unable to say a word.

For the very first time since he had come into the shop, Susan had gotten a good look at him. And she had managed to look past the unshaven face, past the shaggy hair, past the look of melancholy in the expressive, clear blue eyes. And what she saw was affecting her so strongly that she knew there was absolutely no way she could be wrong.

The shabby, downtrodden man standing before her was the same one she had seen in the portrait at the Hollingsworths' mansion! Happy Jack was Michelle and Nicole's uncle!

Nine

"Another long day! I sure am looking forward to getting a good night's sleep!"

As if to demonstrate just how serious she was, Chris stretched her arms into the air, let out a loud yawn, and fell across her bed in a relaxed heap.

Susan looked up from the paperback she was reading in bed and chuckled. "It's funny. I'm not feeling the least bit tired, even though it must be almost midnight."

"You're probably too excited to sleep, after having won all three games of Scrabble tonight," her twin teased. "I wouldn't be surprised if Grandma and Grandpa decided never to play the game with you again!"

Chris leaned over and snapped off the light next to her bed. "Well, Sooz, you can be a night owl if you want, but this early bird has another big day of scooping sweetness into other people's lives coming up tomorrow. Good night!"

With that, she pulled the blankets up over her head.

"Good night, Chris." Susan looked over at her sister and sighed. It was true that the last thing she felt like doing right now was sleeping. She simply had too much on her mind.

Every time I turn around, she thought ruefully, I find out still one more mysterious thing about the Hollingsworth family. More and more questions keep coming up . . . yet I never seem to get any answers!

She turned back to her book, telling herself that it was high time she stopped thinking about the Hollingsworths so much. But she couldn't help smiling as she noticed that she was still looking at the same page she had started reading an hour ago.

I give up! she thought. She put the book on the night table, turned off the light, and, using her sister's determination as inspiration, pulled her blankets up over her own head.

Even lying in the dark, however, trying to get to sleep, she couldn't keep her thoughts from turning back to the Hollingsworths. What exactly was going on over there? If Happy Jack really was Michelle and Nicole's uncle—the supposedly "bad" man who had been banished from their house years and years earlier, so long ago that Nicole could scarcely remember him—what had he done to deserve such terrible treatment? Why did he still live on the island . . . in poverty, no less, even though he was the member of such a wealthy and prominent family? Why had he stolen that jeweled box, something that was worth a great deal of money, no doubt, but was only one of a thousand such valuable antiques?

Then there were all the other questions that had been plaguing Susan ever since she had started working at the Hollingsworths' mansion. The forbidden wing of the house; the redheaded woman who seemed to be keeping herself hidden from an outsider like Susan; that peculiar feeling Susan kept getting as she entered and left the Hollingsworths', the feeling that she was being watched.

None of it makes any sense! she thought over and over, trying to fit all the pieces together but only meeting up with frustration. If only there were some way I could figure out what all the mystery is about. . . .

Finally Susan admitted that she wasn't about to get any sleep—at least not yet. She glanced over at her sister's bed and saw that Chris was fast asleep, probably dreaming about hills and mountains made of ice cream. She climbed out of bed and tiptoed out of the room. After picking up last week's issue of the *Seagull Island Gazette*, which still lay on the coffee table in the living room, she went outside, onto the porch.

Speaking of mysteries, here's *another* one, she was thinking as she settled down into the rocking chair and looked at the headline ANOTHER CHEMICAL DUMP! for the hundredth time. Only this one is a lot more serious than the peculiarities of the Hollingsworth family. . . .

Enough! she finally insisted to herself. Chris and Grandma and Grandpa are right. This chemical-dump mess is something that's really out of my hands. I should just forget it and leave issues like that to people who really can do something about them, people like Charles Hollingsworth.

She tossed the newspaper aside and leaned back in the rocking chair. It was a beautiful night, and from the Stevenses' porch she had a lovely view of the ocean and the lights of Seagull Harbor. The moon was full and illuminated the water before her so that she could actually see the moonbeams playing on the gentle waves. Everything was perfectly tranquil, and for the moment, at least, it felt as if she were the only person in the world.

Susan sat rocking and staring out at the scenic view, and gradually she felt her eyelids growing heavier.

Maybe I'll fall asleep after all, she thought dreamily, relishing the delightful feeling of drifting into slumber.

And then, all of a sudden, she jumped up with a start, all traces of sleepiness gone. Her eyes were as wide as the big yellow moon above, as was the big O that her mouth now formed.

"Oh, my gosh!" she muttered under her breath, her eyes still fixed on the stretch of beach right in front of her.

A small tanker had just moved into her view—the kind of boat used for industrial purposes, a far cry from the pleasure craft that she was used to seeing around Seagull Harbor. It was so large compared to the other boats anchored in the calm waters that Susan's first impression was that some huge monster had just crept up on her.

She stood up to get a better look. As she did, she became aware of a huge dark shadow next to the tanker, a shadow that seemed to be growing bigger as she watched.

"Oh, no!" she cried softly. "*Another* chemical dump! And there's no one else around to see it but me. . . . Ooh, I wish I had a camera!"

Even if she did, she knew, she would never be able

to take a picture that would illustrate clearly what was obviously going on there. No, she was the only witness, as far as she knew, the only person who was watching the third illegal dumping of chemicals in Seagull Harbor.

If only I could see better! she was thinking. True, the waters were somewhat lit up by the moon, and she was fairly close to the ship. Even so, she wished she could get even nearer . . . near enough so she could find out exactly whose boat it was that was polluting the scenic harbor with its chemical waste.

And then, just when she was feeling frustrated about her inability to find out more about what was going on, the boat moved through the water in such a way as to expose to view the huge letters painted on its side. Susan stared as hard as she could, her heart pounding as she realized that this could well be her only chance to find out who was responsible for this horror.

"G . . . S . . . W . . . O . . . or maybe that's a Q . . ." she said aloud, saying each letter as through squinted eyes she attempted to figure out what it was. And then the boat hurried away, its foul deed completed, and she could no longer see its side.

She watched in silence as the boat slipped away, finally disappearing from her view. But her heart was still pounding . . . and her thoughts were still racing.

I actually witnessed the third chemical dumping! she was thinking. And I even have a clue as to who's behind it!

She sat back in the rocking chair, repeating the letters over and over, trying to make some sense out of them.

They must be initials, she was thinking. "G. S. W. Q." But what on earth could they possibly stand for?

She didn't know how long she sat outside, thinking about what she had just seen and what it all meant, knowing that the very idea of sleep was ridiculous. But finally, after having decided that beginning a full-scale investigation of the chemical-dumping problem was going to become her top priority, starting the very next day, she dragged herself out of the rocking chair and went back into the house.

First chance I get, she was thinking as she lay down in bed, I'm going to take a trip over to the offices of the *Seagull Island Gazette* to talk to that reporter, Adam Price. That seems like the obvious place to start in trying to get to the bottom of all this. . . .

And even though she was convinced that she would never manage to sleep until the entire matter of the illegal dumping was cleared up, the next thing Susan was aware of was her sister shaking her gently and telling her it was time to get up.

The next morning, Wednesday, Susan discovered that the Hollingsworth household was buzzing once again. Only this time it was for a *good* reason, rather than a bad one. Preparations had already begun for that Friday night's big charity event, the annual fund-raising ball that Michelle had mentioned the day before.

Susan was just as wide-eyed as Nicole and her sister as the three of them sat glued to the bedroom window all morning, watching as a steady stream of people came into the yard, all of them hired to help make the party a success. A couple who had driven up to the house in a truck with "Rosebud Landscaping Service" written on the side scrutinized every inch of the Hollingsworths' property, it seemed, taking notes in a small spiral notebook as they discussed what they saw with great seriousness. Then came a woman who the girls decided must be the caterer, given the enthusiasm with which she was overheard to cry that one particular spot was the "perfect place for the carving board."

Next a representative from a company that rented tables and chairs showed up, along with a woman from a linen company—no doubt hired to supply tablecloths and napkins. Finally the most exciting thing happened: a huge yellow and white striped tent was set up in the backyard, converting what had previously just been a pleasant garden into the ideal spot for an elegant party.

"Boy, this is going to be some party!" Susan said wistfully. "I only wish I were invited!"

Nicole looked at her in surprise. "Hasn't my aunt spoken to you about that yet?"

Now it was Susan's turn to be surprised. "Why, no. What do you mean, Nicole?"

But before the younger girl had a chance to explain, her big sister interrupted. "Aunt Marion thinks we're too young to be left on our own during an important evening like this one," she said, obviously insulted. "She plans to ask you to baby-sit us that night. To keep us out of everyone's way, I suppose."

"Oh, no!" Susan insisted. "I don't think that's it at all."

"Oh, really? Then why do you think she wants you to be with us during the party?"

Susan thought for a moment, wanting to come up

with an answer that would show Michelle that she was on her side. Despite her intentions of winning the nine-year-old girl over, she felt she had yet to make any real progress. Here, she saw, was a chance to try to break through the little girl's cool façade.

"Because," Susan replied gently, "I think she wants me to see how grown-up you are, getting all dressed up and playing hostess at a fancy party like this one."

The smile that crept over Michelle's face told Susan that she had managed to say just the right thing.

But the excitement at the Hollingsworths' was forgotten the moment Susan left their house. It was time for her to carry out the commitment she had made to herself the night before, to start looking into the *other* mystery that had been plaguing her: the chemical dumpings that had been taking place in Seagull Harbor.

Just as she had hoped, the office of the *Seagull Island Gazette*, located just down the street from the ice-cream parlor where Chris worked, was still open when she arrived there at ten minutes to six. Her luck held out, too; while only a handful of people were still there, Adam Price happened to be among them.

"Mr. Price?" said Susan as she approached the balding man, who was sitting at the gray metal desk in the corner of the single large room that apparently constituted the *Gazette* office.

He looked up from the typed pages he was reading, his expression one of surprise. But when he saw that it was a polite young woman who was seeking him out, his face softened into a friendly smile.

"Well, hello there! Yes, I'm Adam Price. What can I do for you?"

"My name is Susan Pratt, and I'm spending the summer here on Seagull Island. And, um, I've become kind of interested in the chemical dumpings that have been polluting Seagull Harbor."

Adam Price's smile turned to a frown. "Yes. It's a terrible thing, isn't it?"

"Yes, it is. Not only for people like me, who came to spend the summer on a resort island. It's also bad for the environment, not to mention the shopkeepers here on the island who are losing lots of money. . . ."

"You don't have to tell me! I'm the one who's been investigating it for the newspaper, remember?"

"Yes, I know. And that's why I thought I'd start out by talking to you."

Adam Price eyed Susan warily. "What do you mean, 'start out'?"

She raised her chin and took a deep breath. "Well, to tell you the truth, Mr. Price, I have some information that may be of interest to you. Mainly about the *third* chemical dumping. You know, the one that took place last night."

The reporter was silent for a long time. And then, looking at Susan in what she thought was a very peculiar way, he said, "Why don't you pull up a chair, Miss . . . What did you say your name was?"

"Pratt. Susan Pratt."

Once she was sitting down, she poured out the whole story, about how she had been unable to sleep the night before and how she had gone outside to sit on her grandparents' porch . . . and ended up witnessing the third illegal dumping of chemicals into Seagull Harbor.

"Tell me again what you saw on the side of the

boat—or, I should say, what you *thought* you saw," Mr. Price said once she had finished.

"Oh, I'm positive about what I saw," Susan replied confidently. "I distinctly saw several letters. First was a G, then an S, then a W. . . ." Suddenly she thought of something. "Mr. Price, shouldn't you be writing this down?"

Adam Price leaned back in his chair so that he was looking down his nose at Susan—in the same way that both Marion Hollingsworth and her butler Mr. Powell had. She knew immediately that she wasn't going to like whatever it was he had to say.

"Miss Pratt, I'm sure that you really believe that you saw what you're telling me that you saw. But I'm afraid that your account is worthless."

Susan's mouth dropped open. "What do you mean, 'worthless'? I read in the *Gazette* that no one was having any luck finding out who was responsible for the illegal dumping. And here you have an eyewitness, with actual *clues* as to who the culprit is, and you're acting as if—"

But even before she could finish what she was saying, Adam Price stood up as if to signify that their conversation had ended.

"Miss Pratt, I suggest that you leave such important matters to the people who live on this island, rather than butting in where you don't belong. I appreciate your interest, but I really do have to get back to work. Good day!"

Susan just sat there for a few seconds, unable to believe what she was hearing. Why, she had just told the reporter who was investigating this matter some very valuable information—the first solid piece of evidence that anyone had been able to come up with—

yet he was acting as if he couldn't be bothered! It just didn't make any sense. . . .

Even so, she couldn't sit there forever. It was obvious that Adam Price had no interest in talking to her for a minute longer.

She was about to leave, wondering what she should say to this man, when she suddenly heard a reporter sitting at a nearby desk call, "Adam, Charles Hollingsworth is on line three!"

I wonder if he'd be interested in hearing about what I saw last night, thought Susan as she walked out of the *Gazette* office, feeling totally discouraged. *Maybe I'll have a chance to talk to him soon . . . maybe even the night of the party.*

Hoping to lift her spirits, she decided that instead of dwelling on the unpleasant conversation she had just had with Adam Price, she would concentrate on the big charity event she would be attending in just two nights.

What fun it's going to be, going to a party like that, given by Seagull Island's most prominent family! she thought as she strolled down Ocean Street. *True, I'll really only be looking on from the sidelines, since I'll be there as Michelle and Nicole's baby-sitter, after all. But even watching is going to be wonderful. Oooh, I can't wait to tell Chris!*

At that point she found herself right in front of the Seagull Ice Cream Emporium. It was just about the time of day that Chris usually left work, so Susan stopped in, wondering if perhaps she and her twin could walk back to the house together.

"Hi, Neil!" said Susan as she went inside. "Is Chris here?"

"Hi, Susan. As a matter of fact, she just stepped

out. We ran out of sugar cones, and she offered to pick some up at the grocery store and drop them off here before going home. She should be back in ten minutes or so. Care to wait?"

Susan shook her head. "I'd better not. I'm making dinner tonight, and I want to get started right away. I'll see Chris soon enough."

Suddenly she had an idea. "But I think I'll leave her a note. I have some exciting news to tell her, and I'll give her just enough information to get her interested."

Smiling, she took out a piece of paper and a pen. But as she began writing what was supposed to be a playful and mysterious message to her twin, she stopped midway, frozen to the spot.

"Guess who's going to an elegant fund-raising party at the Hollingsworths' Friday night" was what she started to write.

But as she was printing the words, she made a connection that made her heart pound.

Four of the letters in the middle of the name "Hollingsworth" were oddly familiar. And as she printed the letters "G S W O," she realized that the two mysteries that she had been thinking about ever since her arrival on Seagull Island—two mysteries that up until this moment she had been thinking of as two entirely separate issues—were suddenly beginning to look as if they were one and the same.

Ten

"Christine, you and I have definitely got to have a talk!"

Chris was taken aback by her sister's sudden vehemence. As she looked up from the magazine she had been perusing as the Pratt twins sat outside on the porch that Wednesday evening, she was expecting to see a teasing smile on Susan's face, or at least a mischievous glint in her dark brown eyes. Instead, she saw that her sister's expression was one of dead seriousness.

"What is it, Sooz? Is something wrong?"

"Not *wrong*, exactly . . . just incredibly, bizarrely suspicious."

Chris, draped comfortably across the porch's railing, tossed her magazine aside and gave her sister a knowing look. "And I bet I know what this is about, too. It's got to be that weird Hollingsworth family again. Oh, wait a minute; I suppose what you're about to say could also be about the chemical dumping that's been going on in Seagull Harbor. . . ." Chris shrugged. "See that? I guess I'm not such a know-it-all after all. Which is it, Sooz?"

"Actually, it's both."

"Both? You mean today you found out something about *each* of those things?"

"Chris," Susan said earnestly, her eyes narrowing as she leaned forward in her rocking chair, "what would you say if I told you that I was beginning to realize that the two of them are actually related?"

"I'm afraid I don't follow."

"What I'm trying to say is, I'm getting the feeling that the Hollingsworths are the ones behind the illegal chemical dumping."

Chris's reaction to her sister's statement was practically falling backward off the railing. "But Sooz, that's *impossible*! You yourself heard Charles Hollingsworth make that speech, right in front of just about every one of Seagull Island's residents, all about how concerned he was about the dumping! Why, the mayor even put him in charge of the task force that was created to investigate the whole thing!"

"That's exactly how I felt . . . that is, until earlier this evening, when I made a connection between what I saw last night and the name of the family that is—to quote Todd Moore—'Seagull Island's oldest, wealthiest, most civic-minded family.' "

Chris shook her head in confusion. "Maybe this salty sea air is getting to me or something, but I'm afraid I still don't get it."

"Okay. Remember this morning over breakfast, when I told you about what I'd seen painted on the side of that boat last night? Those few letters I managed to make out?"

"Well, sort of. Wasn't it G, W, S, and Q?"

"Either Q or O. I wasn't sure at first. But now I am. Today I started writing you a note about how I'd been asked to baby-sit for Michelle and Nicole during the Hollingsworths' annual fund-raising event, and I realized that that strange combination of letters appears in the middle of the name 'Hollingsworth'!"

"You're right," Chris observed after thinking for a few seconds, picturing the name spelled out in her mind. "In other words, you think that Charles Hollingsworth owns the tanker that's been polluting Seagull Harbor—if not him directly, then some company that his family owns."

"Exactly! I'm not *sure*, of course . . . but I'd give my eyeteeth to find out. And if my suspicions are true, I have a feeling I'm not the only one who knows it, either."

Chris eyed her sister warily. "I take it you're not referring to *me*."

"Nope. Much bigger game, I'm afraid." Susan's voice was low as she continued. "I think that Adam Price knows about it but that he's being paid off or threatened or . . . or *something* in order to keep quiet about it."

"Sooz, that's quite an accusation! Are you sure?"

Susan sighed. "No. I'm not sure. But you should have seen the way he reacted when I told him what I saw last night! And then having Charles Hollingsworth telephoning him like that . . ."

"It's all circumstantial evidence, Sooz. I'm afraid that none of it proves a thing. It's just . . . intuition."

"I know," said Susan glumly. "I need more information or some kind of concrete evidence. And that's why I need to take some drastic action in order to get to the bottom of all this mystery once and for all."

"Drastic action? Uh-oh. Sounds like trouble." Instead of a disapproving look, however, there was already a mischievous grin on Chris's face. "What have you got in mind, Sooz?"

Susan glanced around suspiciously. "How about taking a walk along the beach, Chris? Then I can tell you about my plan."

"Afraid someone may be listening to our conversation?" Chris was teasing as she hopped off the railing and pulled off her sandals in anticipation of their stroll along the seashore.

Her sister, however, nodded earnestly. "You've hit the nail on the head. Did I ever mention that sometimes when I'm going into the Hollingsworths' mansion or coming out at the end of the day, I get the distinct feeling that someone's watching me?"

"Yes, you did. . . . But Sooz, who could it possibly be?"

Susan shook her head. "That's one more thing I don't know, Chris. And one more thing I have every intention of finding out."

Chris looked around and was confident that now that she and her twin were on the beach, walking slowly along the edge of the water on the soft, warm sand, no one would be able to hear them.

"Okay, Sooz. Spill the beans. Exactly how do you intend to find the answer to all these questions you have, about the Hollingsworths and the dumping and the feeling that you're being watched?"

"It's simple. I plan to sneak into the forbidden wing of the Hollingsworth mansion."

Chris reached out and grabbed her sister's arm as if to warn her. "But Sooz! You can't go in there! Marion Hollingsworth told you it's off-limits to you!"

"Which is precisely why I'm so sure that that's something in there that will give me the answers to all the mysteries surrounding the Hollingsworth family!"

Despite her sister's certainty, Chris still wasn't convinced. "I don't know, Sooz. Don't forget what Michelle and Nicole told you. Remember? That the wing of the house is dangerous because it's on the verge of collapsing?"

"If it's so dangerous, then what was that redheaded woman doing in there? Besides," Susan went on, pensively gazing out at the water, "as the days go by, I'm becoming more and more convinced that a *lot of what the Hollingsworths say isn't necessarily true.*

"All right, then. I agree that checking out that wing of the house is probably a good place to start. It does sound as if the Hollingsworths are hiding something, and based on everything you've told me, that does seem like the obvious place to assume that they're hiding it. But how are you going to sneak inside without any of the Hollingsworths knowing about it?"

Even before her twin had a chance to answer, however, Chris had a good idea of what her sister's response was going to be. So she wasn't at all surprised when Susan said evenly, "That, my dear twin—my dear identical twin—is where you come in!"

"Okay, let's hear it," Chris said with mock dismay. "What's the plan . . . and what's *my* role in it?"

"It's easy. This Friday night, that big fund-raising event will be going on at the Hollingsworths'. The place will be full of excitement, with lots of people walking around the house and the grounds. . . ."

"Which provides us with the perfect opportunity to go into places where we're not supposed to go." Already Chris's eyes were shining, reflecting her growing excitement as her sister's scheme was beginning to unfold.

But she grew dismayed as something else occurred to her. "Oh, dear. What about Michelle and Nicole? You *are* supposed to be baby-sitting them all evening, right? You can't just disappear, going off to explore in the Hollingsworths' mansion!"

Susan smiled. "I know. That's where you come in."

Chris was silent for a moment—and then a big grin crept across her face, as well. "Oh, *I* get it! On Friday night there are going to be *two* Susan Pratts at the Hollingsworths', one to watch the girls and one to sneak into the back wing of the house!"

"Now you're catching on. Here's my plan, in a nutshell. We'll both go to the Hollingsworths' dressed as me. My job will be to sneak up to the back wing of the house. I know exactly where to go . . . and if anyone sees me walking around upstairs, on my way up there, they won't be suspicious, since I *am* a Hollingsworth employee, after all. And if they question me about being where I'm not supposed to be, I'll make up some excuse—"

"I know! You can say that you're playing hide-and-seek with Nicole and Michelle!"

"Chris, that's brilliant! Now I know why I chose you as my twin sister in the first place!"

103

Chris laughed. But she quickly grew serious once again. "Uh-oh. I just realized something. If you're going to be running around the Hollingsworths' mansion, that means *I'm* going to be left in charge of Michelle and Nicole!"

"Precisely."

"But Sooz!" Chris wailed. "I don't even *know* them! How will I even know which one is Nicole and which one is Michelle?"

"That's easy. Michelle is the one who never smiles." After dwelling on that sad reality for just a moment, Susan went on. "Don't worry, Chris. I'll fill you in on every single detail that I can think of. It'll be a breeze, pretending you're me."

Chris still looked doubtful.

"Look, it's not as if we've never done this before!" Susan reminded her twin playfully. "I've been Christine Pratt; you've been Susan Pratt. . . . We're positively *experts* at switching identities by now!"

Chris had to agree. With a chuckle, she added, "And we've always been successful at fooling everyone, too. Well . . . *almost* always!"

"Well, this time I have no doubt that we'll be able to carry off our little caper!"

"I sure hope so. And I'll tell you what: whether we find out anything about the Hollingsworths' secret or not, once it's all over, we can go over to the Seagull Ice Cream Emporium for our reward: two double-dip ice-cream cones!"

"That's a wonderful idea, Chris. And not only because it'll be a reward worth looking forward to, either."

Chris looked puzzled. "Why else, Sooz?"

"Because," Susan replied, wearing an impish expression, "you've just helped me think up the perfect name for Friday night's adventure. Since you'll be disguised as me and we plan to celebrate with double-dip ice cream cones, we can start thinking of it as the 'Double Dip Disguise'!"

Chris laughed. "It sounds like fun, Sooz! Now we have to decide what to wear, since we'll have to dress exactly the same, of course. . . . And you have to tell me everything you can think of about Nicole and Michelle. . . . Ooh, this is going to be fun!"

Even as Susan agreed with her sister, however, there were fears nagging at her that she couldn't ignore. It was true that the Double Dip Disguise would be fun. Going off to the Hollingsworths' fund-raising party together; managing to fool everyone; finding out once and for all what was in the "forbidden" wing of the house . . .

But she couldn't lose sight of what it was she was trying to investigate. The Hollingsworths—especially Nicole and Michelle's father, Charles Hollingsworth—were definitely up to no good. And she had taken it upon herself to expose them, once and for all.

For all she knew, Charles Hollingsworth could turn out to be a very dangerous man. He certainly was ruthless and conniving, if it turned out that he was indeed the person responsible for the illegal chemical dumpings in Seagull Harbor—something he could well have been lying about all along. And if he was that kind of man . . . well, there was no telling *what* she would find hidden in his house.

Yes, Susan thought as she and Chris headed back to the Stevenses' summer house to look through their closet and put together two identical outfits for Friday night, the Double Dip Disguise definitely has its exciting side. But I also have to keep in mind that in this little adventure of ours, the stakes are pretty high.

And with that thought, she shuddered.

Eleven

"*Ooh, this is going to be so much fun!*" Chris squealed. It was Friday evening, and the Pratt twins were driving up to the Hollingsworths' mansion in the car they had borrowed from their grandparents. "Not to mention the fact that this is also going to be a real *challenge!*"

"I'm glad you're looking forward to tonight so much," Susan replied, chuckling with amusement. "Especially since you won't exactly be arriving at this party in style!"

She glanced over her shoulder, toward the backseat, the direction from which her sister's muffled voice had come. At the moment, Chris was crouched down on the floor of the car, hidden beneath a blanket. While, as Susan had teased, it was not the most glamorous way to arrive at an elegant fund-raising event, it was an obvious solution to the problem of making sure that no one noticed that not one but *two* Susan Pratts were heading toward the Hollingsworths' this evening.

And that was indeed the case. Tonight both Chris and Susan were dressed in exactly the same clothes—a dark skirt, a plain white blouse, and simple dark shoes—a typical Susan ensemble. It was hardly the kind of outfit that Chris was in the habit of wearing, as she had been complaining cheerfully ever since Susan had decided it was what they would be wearing to the Hollingsworths' party.

"But Sooz!" Chris had wailed. "This is going to be one of the most fantastic parties I've ever been to in my entire life! Can't we come up with something just a little bit more dazzling?"

Susan, however, had stood firm. "In the first place," she had reminded her sister patiently, "you're supposed to be *me* on Friday evening, remember? That means you have to dress the way I usually do. In the second place, Susan Pratt is going to be baby-sitting during this party, not jumping out of a cake. And in the third place, we want to blend into the background, to be careful not to call attention to ourselves. . . ."

"Okay, okay," Chris had grumbled. "You're the boss." Wistfully she had stared at her reflection in the mirror, playing with her hair as she tried to devise some way of dressing up her appearance without violating any of the ground rules her twin had just laid down. "Could we at least wear our hair pulled back?"

"All right," Susan had agreed, laughing. "After all, it *is* a party. And there's no law that says even a Hollingsworth employee can't do something a *little* bit special!"

And so the girls had pulled their hair back on both sides and fastened it with pretty rhinestone barrettes they had picked up at the drug store on Ocean Avenue.

In fact, at the last minute, Susan had bought two extra sets, as well, as one more idea of how to help the evening proceed smoothly occurred to her.

Despite both girls' care in making preparations, however, Susan was experiencing little of her twin's excitement as she walked up to the Hollingsworths' front door after having parked the car on the street, half a block away. Instead, a terrible feeling of dread had fallen over her. She was very worried about carrying off the Double Dip Disguise.

Chris was right; it *was* going to be a challenge. Not only would Chris have to convince both Michelle and Nicole that she was Susan Pratt; she, Susan, would have to do some fast footwork to get into that back wing of the house and take a quick but thorough look around, all without getting caught. Certainly she had done her share of sleuthing in the past, and she had always managed to pull things off just fine. But this time she was dealing with a wealthy, powerful family . . . and the truth was, she was just plain scared.

Still, she held her head up high as she rang the doorbell and waited.

The butler, Mr. Powell, greeted her with his usual, icy formality. "Good evening, Miss Pratt."

"Good evening, Mr. Powell," Susan said with a confidence she didn't really feel. "And it's a lovely evening for a party, isn't it? By the way, I left a surprise out in the car for the girls. I'll be going out to get it in a few minutes, after I've had a chance to say hello."

"Very good," he replied. Already he had lost interest in her, instead turning his attention to a woman in a glittery evening gown and a man in a tuxedo climbing out of the long black chauffeur-driven limousine that had just pulled into the driveway.

Well, I don't think he's about to get in the way of the Double Dip Disguise, Susan thought wryly. He wouldn't notice if there were a *dozen* Susan Pratts!

She went right upstairs to the girls' room, after glancing inside the library and seeing that Marion Hollingsworth was busy scolding the florist, insisting that there were simply too many red flowers and not enough yellow. Michelle and Nicole were already dressed and waiting for her. Susan wasn't at all surprised to see that they were wearing crisp white organdy dresses that looked quite uncomfortable, with their starched skirts and big, puffed sleeves and ruffles around the neck.

"Don't you look pretty!" she said admiringly as she strode into their bedroom. "And so grown-up!"

"Yes, but this dress is so stiff that I can hardly move!" Michelle complained. "Besides, Aunt Marion told us that if we get dirty we'll never be allowed to go to another party again."

"Oh, I don't think she really means that," Susan soothed her, knowing even as she spoke that the woman could well have meant every single word. "Besides, you're not about to get dirty. We'll be really careful, okay?"

"Does that mean we can't eat any chocolate ice cream?" Nicole asked, her blue eyes wide. "I always spill chocolate ice cream on my clothes."

"I'll tell you what," Susan told them after thinking for a few seconds. "Later on, after you've put on your nightgowns, I'll sneak downstairs and get you both some chocolate ice cream. Then you can eat it without worrying about ruining your pretty white dresses!"

The girls looked more cheerful than they had since she'd come into the room.

"But the party's barely gotten started," Susan went on, glancing out the window and seeing that the guests were still arriving. In the backyard she could see a handful of people strolling out of the house, toward the tent, strutting around in their finery. A chamber-music group was setting up in one corner, and the waiters and waitresses who had been hired for the occasion were passing around trays of hors d'oeuvres. While it was still early, it looked like a wonderful party, and Susan could hardly wait to go downstairs so she could get an even better look.

For the next half hour, she and the two little girls sat by the window, wide-eyed, as they watched the party get under way. The music started, strings of yellow lights glowed as the summer sky grew dark, the sounds of talking and laughter and clinking glasses grew louder. Soon the party was in full swing, an event that was a joy to watch. And Susan wasn't the only one who was finding it all enthralling.

"When do we get to go downstairs?" Nicole finally demanded, looking as if she were going to burst if she was forced to wait very much longer.

"Soon, I'm sure," Susan reassured her. "When I talked to your aunt yesterday, she told me to stay with you girls here in your room until she sent for you."

"But that might not be for a long time yet!" Michelle groaned.

"Oh, I'm sure it will be soon," said Susan. "Besides, just think: the later your entrance is, the more dramatic it will be!"

Suddenly, she realized that she had just stumbled

111

upon the perfect opportunity to institute the first phase of the Double Dip Disguise.

"But I'll tell you what. I brought you girls a surprise. Something for you both to wear tonight at the party. If you wait for me here, I'll go down to the car and get it. All right?"

Nicole and Michelle's faces immediately lit up.

"A surprise?" cried Nicole. "You brought us a surprise? Something to wear tonight? Ooh, what is it, Susan?"

"If I tell you, then it won't be a surprise anymore. But you won't have to wait much longer. I'll go get it right now. Just stay here and watch the party . . . and don't move! I'll be right back."

As Susan went back down the stairs, her heart was pounding. After all, this was the beginning of the switch . . . and the beginning of the escapade she had been worrying about for two solid days.

But it's now or never, she reminded herself, nodding at Mr. Powell as she walked out the front door.

"I thought you'd never get here!" Chris wailed, poking her head out from under the blanket as she heard the car door open. "I was about to fall asleep, for goodness' sake! What kept you so long?"

"It's only been about a half hour," Susan replied. "But so far everything's going smoothly. Now, go inside the front door and up the stairs, just like I told you. Remember, the girls' room is the second door on the left. Oh, I promised that later on I'd sneak down and get them ice cream. Don't forget!"

"Don't forget!" Chris moaned. "Sooz, there are about eight billion things I'm supposed to remember! Nicole's favorite doll, the book Michelle's been reading, the drawer they keep the sweaters in . . . How will I ever get through this?"

"Don't worry. You'll do fine." Susan only wished she really believed what she was saying as she glanced around to make sure no one was watching, then helped her twin out of the car. "Here, let me fix your hair. Your barrettes are crooked. . . . Oh, that reminds me! I almost forgot! Here's the surprise you're supposed to bring back to Michelle and Nicole. I told them I was going to the car to get it."

"What is it?" Chris asked, looking at the small package her sister had just taken out of the glove compartment.

"Barrettes, just like ours. I bought two extra sets. I figured that having them to give to the girls would supply me with an excuse to come out here so that we could change places."

"Sooz, you're a genius! Okay. Barrettes, ice cream, second door on the left . . ." Chris took a deep breath. "I'm as ready as I'll ever be!"

"All right, then. Good luck!"

Already, Susan had stopped worrying about her sister's part in the Double Dip Disguise. For one thing, it was out of her hands. Her twin was now on her own. But even more so, she was too busy concentrating on the task before her.

As Chris strolled toward the front door, Susan hid in the bushes, watching until her sister had disappeared inside the house. Then she waited four or five minutes until Mr. Powell was distracted. As he was busy helping a rather stout woman climb out of a car, she slipped inside the front door, unnoticed.

Susan tried to look as if absolutely nothing were out of the ordinary as she headed toward the front staircase. But when she heard someone say her name, she jumped.

"Why, Susan! There you are again!"

She turned around and found herself face-to-face with Marion Hollingsworth. She was about to greet her by saying something friendly like "My, don't you look lovely this evening!" when she realized that not five minutes earlier, Chris, playing the part of Susan Pratt, undoubtedly had said precisely the same kind of thing.

So instead, she just smiled meekly and said,"Yes, here I am again."

"Are you feeling any better?" Ms. Hollingsworth asked.

Susan could feel the color drain out of her face. "I, uh . . . Yes, much better."

"Good. Taking a little walk outside often helps get rid of a headache, I always find. Now I must get back to my guests. . . ."

Susan breathed a sigh of relief. It was also a sigh of gratitude toward her sister, who had apparently paved the way for her entrance by claiming that she had a headache and might well need to "take a little walk outside" sometime in the near future!

Sometimes it really helps to have an identical twin, she thought. We certainly do think along the same lines! I only hope our little charade continues to go as smoothly as it has so far.

Again trying to look as if nothing at all were out of the ordinary, she made her way up the staircase. Then she continued along the hallway, toward the stairs that led to the third floor—and the back wing of the house. She didn't expect to run into anyone up there, and even if she did, she was prepared with the clever excuse Chris had thought up, the one about playing a game of hide-and-seek with Nicole and Michelle.

No, getting caught at this point wasn't her main concern. What she *was* worried about was what she might find up there.

Quietly she sneaked up the stairs, past the solarium, into the corridor that, up until that moment, she had never before dared go into. And her initial reaction was one of disappointment. She found herself in a long hallway that had thick carpeting and dark wallpaper and off which were a half dozen doors. It looked positively ordinary, just like the rest of the house.

Susan hesitated, wondering whether or not she dared start opening some of those doors. But then she remembered that the reason she was there in the first place was to find out what the Hollingsworths were hiding . . . at all costs.

You've come this far, she thought resolutely. There's no turning back now.

She opened the first door timidly, peering inside, almost afraid of what she might find. Once again she was disappointed. It was nothing more than a bedroom, one that looked as if it hadn't been used for a very long time. While it was carefully decorated, with knickknacks on the dressers and pictures on the wall, everything was covered with a thick coat of dust. It looked like a room that had simply been forgotten.

For the first time since she had decided to explore this wing of the house, it occurred to Susan that perhaps she wouldn't find anything at all.

Oh, well, she thought, trying to remain optimistic. I might as well keep trying. Something still might turn up. . . .

But as she opened up two more doors and found nothing but more dusty bedrooms, she began to feel foolish.

Todd was right! she thought. I *did* let my imagination run away with me! There's nothing up here but more rooms. And for all I know, Marion Hollingsworth was telling the truth when she told Michelle and Nicole that this part of the house was in danger of collapsing at any minute. And here I was, all ready to discover something incredible, something that would prove once and for all that Charles Hollingsworth is responsible for all the chemical dumpings, and even to solve the "mysteries" of the Hollingsworth family. . . .

As she stood there, looking at the fourth, perfectly ordinary bedroom, the whole idea sounded so silly that Susan found herself wondering what had ever possessed her in the first place.

She was about to turn around and leave, in fact, when she suddenly heard a noise. It was barely audible and not at all unusual—a thumping, actually, as if someone had dropped something on the floor or placed it on a table. But it was a *noise*, indicating that someone, or something, was close by.

It sounded as if it had come from the next room, the last one on the corridor, way down at the far end.

I'm sure it was nothing, Susan told herself, not knowing whether her skepticism was motivated by her fear of being disappointed again or her fear of what she might find. But whichever it was, she was nevertheless unable to resist walking stealthily down the hall, toward the last door.

She stood there for a long time, listening to her heart pound, feeling every muscle in her body tingle with anticipation. No other noises came from that room, yet the silence suddenly was just as fascinating to her as the noise had been. Slowly she raised her hand to the doorknob, not making a sound, not certain of whether she should go ahead and open the door or just turn around and run.

But her curiosity and determination got the best of her. She placed her hand on the knob and turned it slowly. She half expected it to be locked, yet it moved easily in her hand. She pushed the door open, took a deep breath, and stepped inside.

Her eyes darted about, taking in everything in front of her. What she saw looked like just one more bedroom. Two dressers, a small table, an upholstered chair . . . and a huge bed. When her eyes met up with another pair of eyes, looking at her from a pile of overstuffed white pillows, Susan let out a little squeal.

"Don't be afraid," a kind voice said. "I won't hurt you."

Susan blinked a few times before what she had found actually registered. While it was indeed just another bedroom, this one was different from all the rest, because it actually had a person lying in the bed. She was a very old woman, who looked frail and tired, with her white hair and sad eyes. Susan knew right away that she had seen those sad eyes before. This woman simply had to be related to Happy Jack, Michelle and Nicole's uncle.

"Who are you?" Susan whispered.

"I could easily ask you the same thing," the woman replied, looking amused. "After all, it is you who are the intruder here, not I."

Susan laughed. "I suppose I am. I'm Susan Pratt. I

work for the Hollingsworths. I take care of Michelle and Nicole. . . ."

"Ah, yes. The babies." The old woman nodded knowingly.

Susan was surprised. "They're not babies, ma'am. Why, Michelle is almost all grown-up already. She *is* nine years old. . . ."

"Nine years old!" The old woman looked astonished. "My goodness! Has that much time really gone by?"

Susan crept inside the room, moving closer to the woman. "Since I've told you who I am," she said gently, "perhaps now you'll tell me who you are."

"I am Louise Hollingsworth, of course." When she saw that her response didn't elicit any reaction from Susan, she said, "I am Michelle and Nicole's grandmother."

Susan gasped. "The girls' grandmother! Then what are you doing up here, all alone?"

"Oh, I am not alone," she replied. "I have Sally, after all. She takes care of me."

Susan immediately surmised that Sally was the woman's nurse . . . and that she very likely had bright red hair.

"But why are you up here in this wing of the house? Why don't you spend time with the rest of the Hollingsworths—especially Nicole and Michelle?"

"I wish I could," the woman replied. "But my daughter, Marion, insists that the excitement would be too much for my heart. No, it is best that I stay up here, where it's quiet."

What a dreadful existence! Susan was thinking. Up here all alone, day after day, never going anywhere or seeing anyone . . . And she doubted that watching one's grandchildren grow up could be bad for *anyone's* heart!

Why, then, she wondered, did Marion insist that her mother stay up here, in isolation?

The answer came to her in a sudden flash.

Of course! *This* is what the Hollingsworths are keeping hidden! This old woman, the mother of Charles and Marion and Happy Jack, knows whatever secrets they are trying so hard to keep hidden! And she doesn't even realize that that's what they're doing to her!

"Tell me, Mrs. Hollingsworth. Do you see Michelle and Nicole's father very often?" Susan asked, hoping she sounded casual even though she was so excited she felt she were about to burst if she didn't get the answers to all her questions within the next thirty seconds.

"Oh, no." The woman shook her head sadly. "Jack was banished from the house long ago."

"Jack!" Susan cried, a chill running down her spine. "But I thought that Charles was their father!"

"Oh, no. Of course not. They are Jack's daughters. . . ." Suddenly her eyes narrowed, as if she had just realized something. "Why did you think that Charles was their father?" she asked.

"Because that's what they're telling everyone!" Susan burst out. "Even Michelle and Nicole believe that Charles Hollingsworth is their father! They think that Jack is their uncle!"

The woman shook her head slowly. "Now I understand everything," she said, sounding very sad indeed. "I was hoping that everything had changed, that everything was settled by now. But I see now that the lies have continued. Perhaps that's even the real reason that Marion and Charles have kept me in isolation all these years, while I, of course, am too weak and too sick to do anything about it. . . ."

"What lies?" asked Susan, her voice nearly a whisper.

Louise Hollingsworth took a deep breath, then began to speak. Susan, meanwhile, hung on to every word, scarcely able to believe what she was hearing, yet knowing in her heart that it was all true.

"There had always been a great deal of competition between my two sons, Charles and Jack. They were so different, right from the start. Jack was popular and handsome, so easygoing and friendly. . . . Why, everyone liked Jack. Charles, meanwhile, was always so serious. Ambitious, too, wanting nothing more than to get ahead and make even more money than the family already had. Eventually my only daughter, Marion, took his side. It was terrible, the way the three of them fought.

"And then, once they were grown up, Jack met a beautiful actress, Lucille. They fell in love and married. Charles and Marion were outraged. I, however, came to see that Lucille was really a lovely woman, not at all the fortune hunter those two accused her of being."

The woman in the portrait! Susan realized. The girls thought she was their aunt, when really she was their mother. . . .

"But I was never able to make my other children accept her. Not that Jack and Lucille cared. They were very happy, very much in love. And, of course, they had their two sweet daughters—first Michelle, then Nicole. Besides, we all managed somehow to keep the family business going. The Hollingsworth Corporation continued to thrive, with my husband running it and all three children working for the company.

"But then my husband died. Charles and Marion got hold of his will before it was executed, destroyed it, and somehow forged a new one. Needless to say, Jack was left out of it entirely. I tried to intervene, but Charles was too determined. He wanted nothing more than to ruin his brother. As for Jack, well, he didn't really care. He had his family, and that was all he needed."

Susan just nodded, too enthralled to think of anything to say.

"And then, when Nicole was barely two years old, Lucille died in a car accident. Jack nearly went mad with grief. Who could blame him? But Charles and Marion took advantage of the situation. They convinced the courts that Jack was too unstable to take care of his own children—probably paid off some psychiatrist—and they had the girls taken away from him. That's when he was banished from the house."

The old woman shook her head, and the tears that had been welling up in her eyes slid down her cheeks. "I think the shock was too much for me. I had never been in very good health, and having both my husband and my daughter-in-law die so close together, then having my son thrown out by my other two children, was just too much for me. My heart couldn't stand it, and I became an invalid.

"It was then that Marion and Charles insisted that it would be best if I were shut up in this part of the house, all alone. I thought they were concerned about what was best for me," the old woman finished, her voice now bitter. "But I see now that what they really wanted was to keep me out of their way so that they could continue to keep Jack away from his children.''

"They have managed to turn them against him," Susan offered carefully. "They think Jack is their uncle and that he's very bad. Although Nicole insists that she does have fond memories of him . . ."

"Oh, he loved those girls so much!" Louise Hollingsworth cried. "They meant the world to him!"

Susan suddenly remembered that strange comment that Jack had made in the ice-cream store, the one about how he hoped Chris and Susan's parents appreciated having two daughters. It all made sense now.

As a matter of fact, a lot of things now make sense, thought Susan. And as far as I'm concerned, it's not too late to help Happy Jack get his daughters back, not to mention his share of the family fortune. . . .

Suddenly she remembered that finding out about the Hollingsworth family was only part of her mission. She also wanted to learn about whether or not Charles and the Hollingsworth Corporation could have been responsible for the chemical dumpings.

"Mrs. Hollingsworth," Susan said breathlessly, "something terrible has been happening lately here on Seagull Island. Someone's been dumping chemicals into the harbor . . . and I have my suspicions that it might be the Hollingsworth Corporation that's behind it. Is there any way you could help me find out if Charles has anything to do with it?"

"I wouldn't be the least bit surprised if he had everything to do with it," said Louise Hollingsworth. "But if it's proof you're looking for, I would try his files. His personal, secret ones, the ones that no one ever gets to see. He keeps them stored in the room across the hall, where no one even knows about them except me. Why, not even Marion knows about them!"

Susan smiled despite herself. So the fifth bedroom was also full of surprises—and here she had been on the verge of concluding that this wing of the house would prove to be nothing more than empty rooms!

See, my intuition *was* correct! she thought triumphantly.

"If you don't mind," she said, "I'd like to have a look at those files."

"Be my guest, my dear. Charles may be my son, but I still can't deny the fact that he's grown up to be an evil, coldhearted man. If you can help him get what's coming to him, I'm only too glad to help. I know that he keeps the key to that bedroom on the little shelf right outside the door."

"I'll go see what I can find right now."

As Susan turned to leave the bedroom, in such a hurry that she scarcely bothered to look where she was going, she nearly tripped over someone—someone who had been standing in the doorway, listening to every word. Susan gasped as she looked up and saw a face staring back at her, a face that she recognized right away.

Twelve

Chris, meanwhile, was having problems of her own.

From the moment she first entered the Hollings-worth mansion and found herself face-to-face with a stern-looking woman who simply had to be Marion Hollingsworth, she realized that the Double Dip Disguise was not necessarily going to be as simple as she had anticipated. And then, when she found herself about to enter the little girls' bedroom, she began to think of a thousand different things that could go wrong.

Well, I might end up having to do some fast thinking, she thought with a gulp. But I'll just have to stick with it and do my best. After all, this is no time to leave Sooz stranded.

Throwing herself wholeheartedly into playing the part of Susan Pratt, she sailed into the girls' room, wearing her biggest smile.

"I'm back!" she announced, trying to appear casual as her eyes swept the room. The smaller girl, the one with the long blond hair and the green eyes, just had to be Nicole. That meant the other one was Michelle.

And *that*, Chris thought triumphantly, just has to be the sweater drawer! Maybe I'll manage to get through this after all!

The girl whom Chris had identified as Nicole came running over right away, squealing, "Where's our surprise, Susan? Where is it?"

"I've got it right here, Nicole." Reminding herself that this was the cheerful, fun-loving Hollingsworth girl, she reached into the bag and grabbed a set of barrettes in each hand. "But first you have to pick a hand."

She held out both hands, fists clenched, and watched with delight as the little girl looked at one hand, then the other, earnestly trying to decide which had the surprise in it.

"*That* one!" she cried, having finally made her choice.

"Well, look what I've got here!" Chris opened her hand, then chuckled as Nicole pounced upon the shiny pair of rhinestone barrettes with glee.

"They're *beautiful*, Susan! Just like yours! Oh, will you help me put them in my hair?"

"Of course. How about you, Michelle? Wouldn't you like a set of barrettes, too?"

The older girl glanced over from the window, where she was sitting, "I guess so."

I can see what Susan's been talking about all along, Chris thought as she led the girls over to the mirror and helped them fasten the barrettes in their hair. Why, these two little girls may be sisters . . . but they're as different as night and day!

But Chris didn't have much time to think about that.

125

Just as she was beginning to relax, deciding that this was going to be a breeze after all, things suddenly began to get complicated.

"Sing that song, Susan!" Nicole pleaded as she pirouetted in front of the mirror, admiring her new barrettes.

Chris froze. "Uh, which song, Nicole?"

"You know. The one you always sing. The one about the butterflies and the little birds. . . ."

"I, uh . . . why don't *you* sing it, Nicole? I'd love to hear you sing that song for a change."

Nicole looked hurt as she glanced up at her baby-sitter. "But Susan! You *always* sing that song!"

At this point Michelle came over, her eyes glazed with anger. "Why won't you sing that song, Susan? Don't you like us anymore?"

"Of course I do, Michelle!" Chris's desperation was beginning to show in her voice. "I just . . . uh, I . . . uh, I've got a sore throat. Yes, that's it. A sore throat."

Goodness, I'm practically ready for the emergency room! Chris was thinking with dismay. First I told Marion Hollingsworth I had a headache. Now I've got a sore throat. . . . I just hope the Hollingsworths don't fire Susan because she's too sickly for the job!

Nicole, meanwhile, had taken Chris by the hand. "That's okay, Susan. You don't have to sing if you don't feel good. I know; let's play a game!"

"Great." Chris was relieved. "That's a wonderful idea. What game would you like to play?"

"*I* know!" said Michelle. "Let's play that one with the brownies and fairies."

Chris could feel her cheeks turning red. "Brownies

126

and fairies? I'm afraid I don't remember that one. . . ."

"But Susan!" Nicole protested. "You just taught us that game this morning!"

"Oh, *that* game with the brownies and fairies!" Chris could feel her heart pounding. She only hoped that Nicole and Michelle couldn't hear it, as well. "I'm sick of that game. Don't you think we could think up something else to do?"

Nicole looked crestfallen. Michelle, meanwhile, was eyeing her baby-sitter in a very strange way.

"Surely we can think up something else to do. . . ." Chris repeated. By this point she was really getting nervous. She looked over at Nicole, unable to think clearly and desperate for suggestions.

Nicole was only too happy to oblige. "I know! We could *paint*! Yes, that's what we can do! Oh, Susan, will you make us some of those wonderful pictures of animals you're always making for us?"

"Gee, I . . ." Chris swallowed hard. She was running out of excuses, and she could tell that the girls were beginning to notice. In fact, before she could come up with some comment about how she couldn't paint because her hand hurt, Michelle came over and peered at her through narrowed eyes.

"Wait a minute. What's going on here, Susan? You seem so . . . so *different* from usual! You don't seem to know any of the songs or the games that are our favorites. You don't even want to paint. . . . Personally, I think there's something funny going on around here."

"Well, I just . . . it's only that . . ."

"Hey, you're not Susan!" A look of shock had just

come over Michelle's face. "The girl who was here before was, but *you're* not!"

"That's silly, Michelle!" Nicole insisted. "Of *course* she's Susan! Who else could she possibly be?"

But before Michelle could come up with an answer to an impossible question, a new voice interrupted the tension in the room.

"Girls, it's time for you to come downstairs to the party. Michelle, Nicole . . . and you, too, of course, Susan."

Chris was actually relieved to see Marion Hollingsworth this time.

Saved! she thought with great relief. At least for now!

She hoped that the girls' excitement over finally getting to be part of the festivities that they had been waiting so anxiously to attend would make them forget all about Michelle's accusation. And, indeed, it appeared that Nicole was thinking of nothing else except the party as the two girls followed their aunt down the stairs. But while both Marion Hollingsworth and Nicole happened to be looking in another direction, Michelle turned around and cast Chris a look that told her she had no intention of forgetting her doubts about her baby-sitter's true identity.

So much for enjoying the Hollingsworths' elegant party! thought Chris, groaning inwardly. Here I'd expected to be going to the event of a lifetime, thinking that the Double Dip Disguise was going to be a cinch. Instead, I'm spending the whole time worrying about a nine-year-old finding me out and ruining the whole thing!

Despite her nervousness, however, Chris couldn't help noticing what a wonderful party it was. All the

128

guests were dressed to the hilt, chatting and laughing and having a wonderful time. The strings of yellow lights made the Hollingsworths' lovely garden look magical, and the soft music completed the perfect setting.

Even the food, laid out on a long buffet table, looked magnificent.

Unfortunately, the mere sight of it prompted Michelle to start up again on the one topic that Chris was hoping so desperately would simply be dropped.

"There's the ice cream!" Michelle declared, stopping in her tracks.

She cried out so loudly that several small groups of people nearby stopped talking and turned to look. Marion Hollingsworth, too, turned to see what Michelle was making such a fuss about.

"There are three flavors of ice cream over there: vanilla, chocolate, and strawberry. Tell me, Susan Pratt—which flavor of ice cream did you promise to bring us later on tonight?"

Chris was aware that by now all the people around her had stopped talking and were watching the little drama that was unfolding before their eyes. Even the musicians stopped playing, having lost their concentration as they, too, became aware that something was wrong.

"Michelle," Marion Hollingsworth scolded, taking a step forward, "I'm afraid you're making quite a scene. I don't think—"

"Here, here. What's all this about?" Just then a man that Chris immediately recognized as Charles Hollingsworth came forward, dressed in a tuxedo and looking very concerned that his party wasn't proceeding completely smoothly. He looked at Michelle.

Then, once he saw how upset she looked, he looked over at Chris, his eyes burning with anger over having the evening interrupted.

Chris wished she could just disappear. She closed her eyes, hoping it would turn out she was only having a dream . . . a very bad dream. But when she opened them up again, she saw Michelle and Charles and Marion, all looking at her with fire in their eyes.

"Which flavor, Susan?" Michelle repeated. "Come on. If you really are Susan Pratt, you should have absolutely no trouble answering that simple question!"

"What are you talking about, Michelle?" Charles Hollingsworth interjected. "What do you mean, 'if you really are Susan Pratt'? Is it possible that this girl is an imposter?" Suddenly a flicker of concern crossed his face.

Chris could feel herself beginning to panic. *I've been caught!* Her thoughts were racing wildly. *And if I get caught in this little charade, that means Susan might get caught as well. . . . And for all I know, that could put her in real danger. . . .*

Vanilla, a voice inside her head told her. *Say vanilla. It could well turn out to be the right answer, and you've got to say something. . . .*

"For the last time, what flavor ice cream did you promise us?" Michelle was demanding angrily.

Chris opened her mouth to speak. But before she could get out the word "vanilla," she heard a loud voice call out, "Chocolate!"

She whirled around and saw that Susan was standing at the top of the stairs, calmly gazing down at the crowd that had gathered below.

"I promised to bring you girls *chocolate* ice cream!"

"See?" Michelle cried, sounding triumphant as she pointed at Chris. "I was *right*! This *is* an imposter!"

"Susan!" Nicole gasped. She looked at Chris, then at Susan, then back at Chris again. "Susan, there are *two* of you!"

"Not exactly, Nicole." Susan began walking slowly down the huge staircase. While to everyone else she looked perfectly collected, Chris could tell from the familiar gleam in her sister's eye that Susan knew the answers to more questions than which flavor ice cream Nicole and Michelle had requested.

"We're identical twins," Susan continued. "I'm the real Susan. This is my sister, Christine."

"But why did you pretend to be our baby-sitter tonight, Christine?" Nicole asked innocently.

Susan answered for her sister. "Because it was the only way I could manage to sneak up into the back wing of this house. Where, I might add, I discovered something very interesting. Or, I should say, *someone* very interesting."

Both Marion and Charles gasped.

"What I learned," Susan went on, ignoring the expressions of horror on both their faces, "is that this man"—she pointed at Charles Hollingsworth—"is the person responsible for the chemical dumpings in Seagull Harbor!"

At that point Thomas Jackson, the mayor of the island, pushed his way out of the crowd.

"What's this?" he demanded. "Young lady, that's quite an accusation to make!"

"That's only part of it," Susan went on. "Charles Hollingsworth also paid off Adam Price, the *Seagull*

Island Gazette's investigative reporter, to keep quiet about the facts!''

The mayor shook his head in disbelief. ''Once again, I must say that without any proof—''

''Ah, but I *do* have proof!'' Susan pulled out a handful of file folders that up until that point she'd been keeping hidden behind her back. ''Here, Mayor Jackson, is all the proof you'll need.''

''Let me see those!'' The mayor reached for the files.

''Gladly.'' Susan handed the papers over to the mayor. ''And if those aren't enough, I can provide you with an excellent witness, someone who'll be pleased to fill you in on all the details of Charles Hollingsworth's less-than-honest business career.''

''Now, wait a minute,'' Charles Hollingsworth growled. ''If you think anyone is going to believe the lies that somebody is prepared to tell—''

''I've never told a lie in my life!'' piped up a high-pitched yet feisty voice. Another figure had just appeared at the top of the stairs, a frail-looking old woman in a robe who was leaning heavily on the arm of her smiling red-haired nurse. ''And I'm not about to start telling them now. Go back to your party, all of you! You may as well enjoy the rest of it, since if I have my way, this house and everything in it will belong to my son Jack soon enough.''

''Do you mean Happy Jack really is your son?'' Chris cried.

A cry of surprise rose up from the crowd. Just about everyone on Seagull Island knew Happy Jack—and the idea that he was related to the Hollingsworths came to them all as news indeed.

"Yes, he is," Louise Hollingsworth replied. "And that's just the beginning. I have a lot to say, now that I realize I've kept silent for much too long. Not entirely through my own doing, I might add." She cast a cold look at her daughter, Marion, who stood at the foot of the stairs, too shocked to say a word. "But before I say anything else, I want to hold my two little granddaughters."

"Grandma?" Nicole blinked, and then slowly a smile crept over the face. "You mean you're my grandma?"

"Grandmother!" Michelle cried, running up the stairs. "Oh, Grandmother, it's really you! I remember now . . . !"

There were tears in the old woman's eyes as she hugged her two granddaughters, glancing up only long enough to give Susan a look of gratitude.

"Boy, what a night!" Chris flopped across the red velvet couch in the Hollingsworths' library, exhausted. "I had no idea that the Double Dip Disguise was going to turn out to be such hard work!"

"Yes, but it was such a success," Susan reminded her, sitting down in a soft upholstered chair opposite her. "Not only did we spill the beans on Charles Hollingsworth—*and* Adam Price—but we reunited Michelle and Nicole with their grandmother."

"*And* their real father," Chris reminded her. "You know, Sooz, when you told me about that funny feeling you kept getting every time you went into or out of this house, the feeling that you were being watched, I thought you were just getting carried away. I never dreamed that Happy Jack spent practically all his time watching this place, trying to catch a glimpse of his daughters. Did you see his face tonight when we brought him in here and he saw Michelle and Nicole for the first time in almost five years?"

"That was really something, wasn't it?" Susan agreed wistfully. "Yes, it's so sad that he had to live without them all these years. Moving to this island, living in poverty the way he did, just so he could be near them, hoping that at least he'd be able to see them every now and then. Even taking that jeweled box the way he did, just so he'd have at least *something* to help him remember his old life!"

"But now, thanks to you, not only will he get his daughters back, but it looks as if he'll get his share of the Hollingsworth fortune, too! Now, *that's* what I call living happily every after!

"That," Chris went on with a twinkle in her eye, "plus seeing his evil brother, Charles, go to jail because of those illegal chemical dumpings he was responsible for. You know, Sooz, you really accomplished a lot tonight. You deserve a lot of credit!"

"Oh, I couldn't have done it without Louise Hollingsworth. *And* Sally. Why, she gave me quite a start when I found out she'd been listening to my conversation with Louise. But I figured out right away that she'd be on our side. After all, for years she'd been helping Nicole and Michelle sneak out to have come fun, the way she did the night of the Fourth of July band concert."

"Well, the girls won't be needing her to do that anymore," said Chris. "I'm sure Jack will provide a much happier family life for Michelle and Nicole than their awful aunt and uncle ever did. A lot of things will be changing for them now."

"And I have a feeling that Michelle will be changing, too," Susan said. "I understand now that the reason she was always so angry at the world was that she believed deep down that her real father had deserted her. She was old enough to remember what had happened but too young to understand why. Up until now she never had any way of knowing the truth. With her real father back, and the chance to be part of a loving family once again, I have no doubt that she'll be just as happy as Nicole in no time."

"Speaking of the time," Chris interjected, "it's getting late. What do you say we say good night to Louise and the girls and be on our way? Don't forget; tomorrow is Saturday, and I plan to squeeze in a full day of fun!"

"That sounds like a worthwhile goal," Susan chuckled, getting up out of her chair. "Although now that I'll be working for Louise and Jack Hollingsworth, I'll be able to take the girls out and start having much more fun *during* the week, too. From now on I'll be going to the pool, bicycling . . . doing all the things with Michelle and Nicole that they weren't allowed to do before, when their aunt and uncle were trying so hard to keep them away from their real father!"

"I hope you'll bring them over to the Seagull Ice Cream Emporium, too," said Chris, dragging herself off the couch. "Hey, that reminds me! You and I have a reward coming to us!"

Susan was baffled for a few seconds, until she remembered. "Oh, of course! Our double-dip ice-cream cones! All right, we'll do our celebrating tomorrow, the very first chance we get. There's only one problem." Susan pretended to frown. "If we're

135

going to treat ourselves to some ice cream, what flavor should it be?"

Chris and Susan looked at each other, then burst out laughing.

"Chocolate!" they cried in unison. Then they slung their arms around each other and, walking side by side, headed for the door.

About the Author

Cynthia Blair grew up on Long Island, earned her B.A. from Bryn Mawr College in Pennsylvania, and went on to get an M.S. in marketing from M.I.T. She worked as a marketing manager for food companies but now has abandoned the corporate life in order to write.

She lives on Long Island with her husband, Richard Smith, and their son Jesse.